DIARY OF
DISBELIEF

SUSAN KAY BOX BRUNNER

DIARY OF
DISBELIEF

Published by FWB Publications, Columbus, Ohio

Published in the United States of America

ISBN: 978-1-940609-74-4
1. Fiction / Romance / General
2. Fiction / General
16.11.16

Acknowledgments

ROSEMARY, YOUR FRIENDSHIP and support has meant the world to me.

And Dustin, thank you for a good eye in photographing me.

1

DR. JOEL TAYLOR Wright walked into his study and sat in a swivel mahogany chair where he unwrapped the unidentified package. It had been sent to him through the partials post. He checked the outside wrappings and there was not a trace from whom or where the package came from and he didn't find any note of any kind inside. Dr. Joel Taylor Wright touched the worn leather diary and began to read from its fragile, aged pages. He admired the skilled penmanship used. As the words unfolded, the writings alleged that the great-great-grandfather, on his father's side, was named Dr. Zachary Taylor. He was also a captain in the war of 1812. His penned words and findings on his life after the war shared his commitment to the study on brain patterns. And, to Joel's surprised when he flipped farther back into the dairy, he found some very private and personal information, of places, people, and events, that Zachary Taylor recorded before the Civil War. Joel let out a long breath, then read on. Recorded was that Dr. Zachary Taylor lived in Kentucky during 1815–1850. He had owned an operable tobacco farm and favored a female slave named Serafine. And that his wife, Margaret Taylor, turned her head when a blue-eyed boy child from the slave woman was brought into their house, as her husband's son, and was raised as theirs. Joel shook his head in disbelief for, if the wording in the diary was true, that child would have been possibly his great-grandfather, William Taylor.

Joel yawned and his eyes watered. He was tired after pulling two double shifts at the hospital for the fourth time in a week. "Too many doctors want to party. Their priorities just aren't in their life's work." He rubbed his neck and said, "Up until now I haven't minded all the extra shifts, but I'm finally in a good place with success and notoriety. All through my hard work. I hold a top position, I'm wealthy, and am requested at all the movers and shakers' society circles." Joel's blue eyes blinked for the third time. He closed the diary and left his desk, going straight to bed, but his sleep was not sound. Joel tossed and turned from the disturbing words found in the diary. When he opened his eyes, it was still dark outside. Joel sat on the bed's edge with a dull headache. He stretched, then walked into his modern kitchen and made a strong pot of coffee. There, he enjoyed the quietness of his place. And thought, *Evidently, I come from a long line of men, who were either committed in the fields of research, or as a community doctor, or they specialized in areas, as surgeons.* Lifting his cup and sipping, he then voiced, "And that's not counting their well-kept secrets for five generations." Joel shook his head in disbelief and reached for the aspirin bottle. Had his forefathers frolicked outside their marriages, and with their own slave girls. Adding coffee to his cup, he walked to the wall of windows and stared out. "Well, it's possible that I've inherited the family traits and skills, and that I may not be as Caucasian as I was raised to believe. My, how life can change on a dime!"

Back in the kitchen, Joel refilled his coffee cup and thought, *There's one thing that all the ancestry of men seem to have in common, and that was the art of science and the strong belief in the divine, as in healing.* He said, "I've witnessed too many patient cases without an answer, except for the Great I Am."

Joel rinsed out his cup, dried it, and placed it on the open shelf, and reviewed his life. "I attended Yale University at the request of my father, and after a year I transferred to the Ohio State University, and enrolled in the study of cardiology. Five grueling years passed, and then I graduated with honors and was first in my class." He went into the living room and said, "But I accepted a doctorate post in Boston at the Boston Ben's Hospital, they offered me more money." He chuckled. "I devoted my life to heart surgery and was nominated best cardiologist doctor three years in a row. And I wasn't surprised that after another five years, a call came from the Ohio State University Hospital for my employment. With a lot more money and a titled position. Yes, I had finally made a name for myself. Head cardiologist, lead surgeon. That was the best decision I ever made."

He stretched, and realized it was now midmorning and time for a shower. Joel turned the hot water on and spread his hands against the shower wall, and let the cascade of water rain over him. Joel was feeling like a new man. With towel around his waist, he stood before the mirror, viewing his six-foot-four, milky-white body, with broad shoulders, and his abs showing defiant indent. "It pays to go to the gym." After combing and hand-styling his wavy blond hair, Joel selected a custom-made suit. All his clothes were tailor-made, and he carried himself with pride. Adjusting his tie, he said, "Does it really matter, my origin, or is it anyone's business, for that matter? I appear the same." He glanced at the stack of society invitations, smiled, and knew his fame, power, and his acquired monies had opened all the doors of his opportunities. True, he had worked hard, but then he enjoyed the niceties of life, and that included him being a confirmed bachelor of thirty-four years of choice. He loved living in the Columbus Wright Heights, High-Risers, named after his mother and her charitable works.

His cell phone jingled. Joel reached for it and recognized the caller. He let the message go to voice mail, for it was a fellow surgeon calling off from work again. That doctor was defiantly a partier, wanting Joel to cover his shift. He would definitely have to talk with Dr. Donavan, he decided, for pulling double or even single shifts for a fellow doctor had run its course. Joel had made it to top billing and was in a great place to call the shots.

⚜

Twenty-four hours later, with six successful heart surgeries, a sudden flow of skateboard causalities, and calming down a child with a cut finger, Joel ended his shifts. He went into the hospital's doctor's dressing room to shower. It felt good to be in his business suit after work, before leaving the hospital, and Joel was thankful to have the next day off. He drove his Porsche back to the high-riser and checked his unopened week's mail. A certified letter was stuffed among the stack of envelopes. He ripped it open before reaching his office. It was his father's attorney, requesting his presence, for the will reading. Joel let out an audible sigh, knowing he would relive his losses all over again and would have to will down his emotions and be like a wooden soldier.

In the quiet of his place, he recalled how just three months prior he had received that dreadful phone call. He was almost out the hospital door after his shift when an overhead page for his name came. He headed to the nurses' station and was handed the phone. "Dr. Joel Taylor Wright speaking,"

"This is Dr. Tate Pratt, I'm a coworker of your father's. We were working on an assignment and had just made a breakthrough in the research laboratory. Your father made a piercing cry and mentioned he was having some stomach pains. He even joked about something he must have eaten when the pains became more severe. It was late, so I rushed him over to the ER, where he had routine blood work, an x-ray, and a stomach biopsy done. Everything appeared normal. Your father was in the recovery room and woke screaming. They rushed him in to surgery, and while still on the operating table his lower intestine bowel twisted and—I'm sorry, Dr. Wright, but your father passed away. You were listed as next of kin. Sir, he'll be a great loss to the world, both as a man and doctor. His research in brain patterns was remarkable."

The proper words were spoken between the doctors and then their lines were silenced. Joel hung his head once again in disbelief. His powerful, authoritative, driven father was dead. Joel made the necessary arrangements to be scheduled off from work and flew to Kentucky—him in first class, and his father in cargo in a pine box. After arriving at his parent's home, he helped with his father's funeral arrangements, and during his three-day stay, his mother had several talks with him. One was her upcoming trip to New Orleans. She sounded fine and even happy under the circumstances. He wished her well and they promised to stay in touch. Joel left his parent's home and headed back to Ohio and his work.

Not even a week later, he received another phone call. This time it was from his old nanny and his mother's housekeeper. She sounded out of breath. "Lands of mercy, Dr. Joel," she said, sniffling. "When I come from the marketplace this morning, I found your mother still in bed, and she was dead. She looked so peaceful. Dr. Joel, I'm so very sorry."

"Ms. Desiree." He closed his blue eyes, breathed out, then said, "Thank you for calling. I'll fly out this afternoon and make all the necessary arrangements and calls for mother's being when I get there. Now you take care of yourself." When he arrived, the house phone was ringing off the hook and Desiree handed him a stack of messages. That day and night was a nightmare. After funeral arrangements were made, a florist was called, and then the society people and the list of boards his mother served on, he discovered he needed to make an appearance on his mother's behalf at a ladies' brunch, where she held a speaking engagement too late to cancel. What did he know about gardening and flowers? He made a quick Internet research, did what he knew best around a flocking group of cackling women, spoke little, smiled a lot, and hopefully charmed them.

On the day of the funeral, people who had known Elena Wright Taylor, for a day or for years, from the community, fundraisers, civic clubs, and church came together for her traditional service. Then afterward, everyone gathered at the house where Joel and Desiree hosted the remembrance meal. It was hours later when everyone left and his jaws ached from all the talking.

The next day sitting at the kitchen table, he asked Desiree to still maintain the house, until things were sorted out, stating he would continue her wages. She agreed. He made necessary calls and sent e-mails to his work, putting the fires out even in his absence. The next morning after coffee, Joel booked a flight to Ohio. He couldn't leave fast enough from his parents' house. Joel immediately reported to work and rested in his doctorate skills. Not even ten days later he was notified by a phone call from the funeral director that his mother had died from heart failure. He ended the call and held the silent receiver in his hand. Joel was in disbelief. He wasn't even aware that his mother had had a weak heart. He finally hung up the phone receiver and with head in hands cried, "How could I've not seen the signs…"

Joel shifted in the seat in the waiting room of his parents' attorney where his mind flashed back in time to when he was a boy. The attachment he felt for his nanny, Ms. Desiree. She was kind and loving. Her words still touched his heart: "You're handsome, Joel, you're smart, and you're kind." His thoughts shifted to his father, Charles Taylor, who had been a wealthy, starched, driven, military man, and a known brain research doctor. Dr. Charles Taylor was a very reserved traditional soul. He was well respected in the community, nationally, and worldwide, and notably a family man, but there was something missing in that department. Joel remembered as an eight-year-old child holding his father's hand, dressed in a suit and tie, a mime of his father, and saying good-bye to his nanny. He stood like a tin solider and then entered the car, waiting to be sent away to a prestigious boarding school. And, strangely, Joel was permitted to come home only on certain holidays. His days remained at the military boarding school until he reached college age. His years of schooling continued, and there is where he realized that his father was a workaholic. As was his grandfather, and his great-grandfather. The words penned from his great-great-grandfather revealed that they as men drove to be well known as doctors in their research and surgical fields.

His thoughts shifted, and reflections of his savvy mother, Elena Wright Taylor, came to mind. She was tall, slender, and elegant, with strong facial features softened by her massive blond curls and her almond-shaped, sky-blue eyes. Elena Wright Taylor was a very musically inclined person. She played the viola, the flute, and the piano. He enjoyed her playing when he would be home for the holidays. His parents mostly lived a quiet, hushed life unless by society's request they host a social event, project, or fundraiser. He heard his name. "Dr. Joel Wright."

The attorney stepped forward, introduced himself, and offered his hand. After they shook hands, the attorney asked Joel to be seated. "Would you care for a drink of liqueur or coffee?"

Joel refused both and smiled. He listened as his parents' joined will was read, and let out a long breath. He had inherited a large sum of stocks, bonds, and monies from two insurance policies, his mother and father's. Then there was a Southern plantation his mother owned, in Mississippi; his parents' suburban house, in Kentucky; and an apartment his father evidently owned in the campus area and used when he was required to be at the Ohio State University's laboratory for his research study. Joel was shocked into reality when handed a sealed envelope holding a CD. The instructions were for him to view the CD on his thirty-fifth birthday, and that was in two months. He had questions building about his father and mother, but the attorney gave his condolence then handed Joel the legal document, which also included a list of contact names for two of the three unknown sites he had just inherited. Reeling from all the news, Joel followed form, stood, shook hands with the attorney, and left his office more confused and yet quite wealthier than before he had entered the building.

He breezed into the hospital with determination and met with his surgical staff and the hospital personal. His shifts were covered, and Dr. Donavan was on final warning about his too many missed shifts. Joel needed a three-month leave of absence. Driving to his high-riser, he packed lightly and made the same-day flight arrangements, trying to at least come to terms with his parents' news. Once again he returned to his childhood home in Kentucky.

It was late afternoon when Joel arrived. The housekeeper greeted him with a curtsy and pulled him in for a hug, shaking her head, sniffling. After a few brief moments, Desiree walked toward the kitchen and said, "Have you eaten, boy?"

His eyes roamed the house as he walked room by room. Everything appeared the same in his parents' ten-room house. It was so formal, furnished with antiques, nothing of his modern taste. "So much stuff!" He glanced in the kitchen's direction. "No, Desiree, I haven't eaten. I'll be there in a little while." He walked into his father's home office and a chill ran up his spine. He didn't recall the time needed to box up his father's life's work or exactly when he had called a courier service to transport the boxes to his high-riser. Much time would be needed to think and sift through all his father's work files.

In the kitchen, he enjoyed the hearty meal and the black coffee set before him. Next, Joel contacted the state's museum and an auction house, which agreed to come to his newly acquired suburban home. He set the time for later in the day. Joel worked for several hours, selecting things to give to Desiree, and when dinner came he enjoyed a light meal with her. They agreed she would stay on until the house was sold, and Joel assured the aged Desiree she would continue receiving a salary until her death. She was like family. She could only nod, sniffle, and fluff her apron.

The doorbell chimed, and a teary-eyed Desiree answered. She announced the museum personal, Ms. Shelly Rife. She and Joel went about his mother's furnishings, whatnots, artwork, custom-made jewelry, and aged musical instruments. After some time of bartering, Joel granted a few paintings and a necklace, earrings, and bracelet set, titled "Blue Jewelry," to the museum, gifted from his mother. Ms. Rife offered to buy several pieces of art outright. He agreed. The doorbell chimed a second time. Joel walked with Ms. Rife to the door after arrangements for pick-up on the tagged artwork and jewelry were made. They bid farewell.

In walked the representative from the auction house. Carl Cally touched and held up different whatnots, nodding, and remarked, "These will bring in thousands of dollars with the right people. Are you sure you want to part with the art and furnishings?"

"I've tagged what I want and I'm listing the house with a realtor, soon."

They agreed on a date when the auction would be held, November 12.

Joel also tagged other precious pieces for himself, a key chain whistle, a Swiss Army knife, and a pocket watch his father had received from his own father that dated back to the 1850s, according to the diary. Truth be known, it was probably passed down from his father, Joel's great-great-grandfather, Zachary Taylor. He stepped outside for a brief moment for a breath of fresh air and inhaled deeply.

A few minutes later, he walked into his mother's private bedroom. It was lovely and feminine. He toyed with a petite ladies' ring, a thin gold band embracing an opal setting. It was her birthstone and so beautiful. He rummaged in her special jewelry box and discovered an intriguing wedding ring set, handcrafted and boldly designed with silver. He never recalled her wearing it. Joel reached up and pulled down the hidden ladder which led to the attic. He found a trunk containing his toys: superheroes, trains, trucks, and a ragged doll. A box sat at the bottom. It held his baptism clothing, a child's gold cross, and a Spanish-looking boys' outfit. A note dropped to the floor. Joel stooped and picked it up. It read: *From your heritage on the Creole side.* He shook his head in disbelief and placed everything back inside, closed the lid, and hauled the trunk to his rental car. He looked toward the heavens, shaking a fist. "Who am I?" Joel returned to the house, drank a cup of black coffee, hugged his old nanny Desiree, and thanked her for his care so many years ago. He said, "You're the only woman I've ever loved."

Although the hour was late, he left from his Kentucky home and drove toward Mississippi. Joel's eyes burned and his head ached and he was sleep-deprived. He pulled off the side of highway and slept five hours. Joel shaved in the car, and two hours later on the outskirt of town, he saw a sign leading him to his mother's estate in Jefferson County. Another hour and a half and he stopped to view the land. As far as his blue eyes could observe and travel, north, south, east, and west, the plantation land continued. And appeared to be in operation.

Upon arrival, he tapped on the huge door's gold knocker. The massive door was swung open, and he was greeted with sincere warmth as he entered the house filled with Southern charm. A few hellos were made and regrets for his losses. A full-sized busty woman curtsied, and introduced herself. "My name is Elsa, plantation housekeeper and overseer in charge, sir. Welcome, Master Wright."

He slightly bowed and offered his hand. He couldn't help noticed how tall, brown, and very well rounded she was. She wore a smile from ear to ear. Smoothly, a burly, darker male servant carried in his luggage, and a young boy tugged on the housekeeper's apron and whispered into Elsa's ear.

She said, "Dr. Wright, you're to follow the lad outside where there's a saddle horse waiting for you."

He removed his suit coat and tie, which Elsa received. Joel then let the lad lead the way. On horseback, Joel adjusted his legs in the saddle and rode for hours, viewing field after field of the standing sugarcane. "Wow" was his only word. The hot winds crossed his face; quite a contrast from Kentucky's climate. His horse seemed to know the much-traveled trail. Joel turned with the horse and headed in another direction. Suddenly before him appeared row after row of never-ending ripe-to-pick cotton. He heard mooing in the far distance. "I'll need to cover that acreage and see the cattle aspects too, but later." Joel again was in disbelief. The plantation went on for miles. His newfound life was hard to digest and totally foreign to him. After he returned to the barn and walked into the plantation house, Joel was taken aback. The helpers, as well as the plantation's chief cook, and all the servants including the greeter doorman but except for the foreman, were apparently of slave descent. Joel blotted his forehead; it was if he had stepped back in time, to another era. Chuckling, he thought, *Had Rhett Butler felt this way stepping into Tara?*

2

His attention returned as he heard someone call him by his given name. "Joel Taylor Wright, sir, your room is ready and you luggage has proceeded you."

He nodded, smiled, and breathed, "Thank you."

"Sir, supper will be served promptly at six o'clock." The man in the tailored long-tail black suit asked, "Is there anything else you require?"

"Which room is mine?"

A female servant bowed and joined him on the grand stairway. She opened the door to his bedroom.

Joel asked, "Is anyone else staying here besides me?"

She nodded, and said, "A woman, a friend of your mother's." She smiled and turned toward the stairway.

Joel's eyes widened. He closed the door. "What friend of my mother's?" He raked his neatly groomed blond hair and stretched his tired eyes over the room. The handcrafted four-post bed was massive and so was the matching dresser apparently from the 1800s. The décor had his mother's design all over it. He walked into the adjoining bathroom and saw a claw-footed tub, a counter holding a basin with a pitcher of water beside. "Where's the toilet?" He shook his head, adjusted his Rolex watch, changed into a dark gray suit, black shirt, with a gray-striped tie. Slapped on some Dior Homme cologne, slipped on his shoes, and graced the steps. In the formal dining room, his breath caught when he noticed the young, curvy woman who was the alleged friend of his mother's. *Perhaps of Spanish descent.* She turned. Her dark brown eyes gazed at him and they just sparkled. She stood and walked toward him, smiling with red, red lips. "Hello, you must be Joel. My name is Lolita Aime, your mother and mine have told me so much about you."

He inhaled quickly and said, "I'm sorry, I'm at a loss, but I am Joel, Dr. Joel Taylor Wright." He stretched his hand forward, but she stepped closer and hugged him. Oh, he needed a hot mug of coffee and now! He pried her soft hands free—she smelt so fresh and sweet—and he sidestepped her, placing the table between them. *What was it about this woman?* Clearing his throat, said, "Let's enjoy our meal, then we can talk afterward." He smiled at least, hoping it didn't look like a snarl, and was relieved that the room was dimly lit. After dinner, he stood and offered his arm (as was the custom), and placed his other arm behind his back. Joel matched her step by step into the drawling room, holding back his stride, with her gracing his side. He noticed her head just touched his chin, but what really caught his attention was the red laced tight bodice dress with a full, rustling skirt. Joel saw that she was seated, then bowed. Turning toward a straight-backed chair, he audibly let out a held breath. What *was wrong?* Women didn't affect him with their beauty, but still he stole another glance. *Ms. Lolita Aime was nothing, but dangerous!* Muttering under his breath, "Intoxicating…"

A male servant entered the room, white–gloved, and asked, "Dr. Wright, would you care for a drink?" And not waiting for an answer poured him a generous amount of tea-colored substance. A female servant dressed in black with a white apron entered the room, carrying a tray holding a china cup on a saucer, and presented it to the attractive woman. He usually didn't drink, but just this once it might take the chill from his body. A quick tilt to the head, a chug, and the golden liquid burned going down, but it was warm, and as he eyed the young female, who was smiling, he thought, *Yep, definitely warmer.* Sitting spine–straight, she said, "As I said, my name is Ms. Lolita Aime and I'm from New Orleans. When your mother hadn't arrived at mother's B & B as planned, I was sent here to do a follow-up. You see, sometimes Mrs. Elena Wright Taylor came to the plantation before making her trip to New Orleans. I'm sorry, um, Mr. or Dr. Wright, but I only found out about your loss when I arrived here two days ago." She licked her lips.

"Ms. Aime."

"I insist you call me Lolita. Yes, you were saying?" She folded her hands in her lap. He crossed his foot over his other leg.

"I knew my mother was planning on a visit to New Orleans, but not any of her arrangements. So, tell me, Lolita?"

She nodded, eyes perked.

"Remind me how our mothers made their acquaintances?" He smiled.

She took a sip of tea then spoke. "Charlotte Tomas was your mother's grandmother. Her maiden last name was Wright. She met and married a Mr. Tomas. They lived in New Orleans and owned a huge estate. Now, my grandmother migrated from Spain, her name, Carolynn Perce, who stopped at the estate and stayed. She eventually bought half of Charlotte Tomas-Wright's estate, and they both came to an agreement to turn the lovely estate into a bed-and-breakfast. That's where my mother was born, as was I." She lifted the china cup to her mouth and sipped. "But before she was a Tomas, your great-grandmother, Charlotte, unknown to the family, became intrigued with a young buck from the Blackfeet Indian tribe. Things happened, and she became his squaw. The young buck was killed a year after Charlotte's disappearance and she chose to return with her light-gray-eyed blond-haired daughter to the then estate. She named her child, Margaret Wright. Years into her adult life, she met a Frenchman who stayed at the B & B and they had a whirlwind courtship. He promised to come back for her after the war was over. But the war ended and he never returned. Margaret gave birth to your mother, who claimed she was Creole, and named her Elena Wright. One day, another Frenchman came to the B & B, a friend of her lost lover's, and this Frenchman asked for her hand in marriage. They married. Margaret had another child, a male." She stood. He followed in like manner. Lolita motioned for him to sit and brought her tea and sat across from him. "Joel, your mother was sent to Paris to a renowned boarding school. It was wintertime when your mother returned home as a graduate.

"Years ago, my mother and yours had become fast friends. Well, Elena had a hard time fitting in at the B & B, and as it happened that same year, a handsome boarder stayed at the B & B. Your mother twinkled when she met the stranger." She took another sip. "Oh, I just love their story. It's so romantic," clasping her hands to her chest, and her dress rustled. "Your father, Lt. Dr. Charles Taylor, had served with Charlotte's husband, Captain Tomas. And the captain insisted whenever the lieutenant was on leave that he stayed at the B & B. So when the dashing Lt. Dr. Charles Taylor received a two-week pass, he came and stayed at the B & B. The lieutenant doctor became smitten with your mother and insisted they be married by the following spring. The Lt. Dr. Charles Taylor was twenty-six years old, and your mother had just turned twenty-one." Lolita stood. She sat her cup on the tray and glanced over at Joel and asked, "Do you ever get tired of hearing about their great love?" Her dress swished as she turned.

Joel took her hand and said, "You do have a way with spending your words." He leaned in and kissed her cheek and said, "Interesting. Good night, Ms. Lolita Aime." Smilingly, he walked briskly to the stairway and didn't stop until he was in his room. His mind was whirling in disbelief. He said, "All this history, my parents' meeting, it's another thing I didn't know. And *romantic* isn't a word I would use for them, it would be more like *accomplished*." He folded the covers back and slid into bed.

Sleep came and went. Joel bolted upright, hearing his bedroom door squeak.

"Sorry, Dr. Wright, just bringing in your 6:00 a.m. coffee."

"When will breakfast be served?"

"Breakfast is from 5:00 to 7:00 a.m...." She backed from the room, closing his door. Joel edged from bed, poured a cup, and enjoyed its rich flavor. After another sip, he stretched, then washed up and shaved. After he was dressed in suit and tie, he placed a direct call in to the attorney's.

A groggy voice answered, "Hello, do you know what time it is?"

"This is Dr. Joel Wright. Sir, what knowledge do you have about my mother's plantation?"

Yawningly said, "Dr. Wright, flip to page 104. I presume you're asking about the loss-profit sheet."

"Yes, among other things. Found it. Thanks, and have a good day. Sorry to have bothered you." The lines silenced. Joel poured another cup of coffee and saw the plus figures shown in the three areas of the plantation's operation. It appeared that his mother had hired a Frenchman, Felix, to oversee the land. He touched his smart phone and googled the name. There were two Felixes listed. One ninety-seven years old, and the other man was dead. The later man had migrated from France to New Orleans, then to Mississippi. He rubbed his chin. "Hum, wonder how my mother knew him?" Joel left his room, graced the steps, and walked into the dining area where breakfast was served smorgasbord style. A few ranch hands were seated at the long table along with Lolita. "Hello." She patted the seat next to hers.

He smiled and unfolded in the chair. *I'm out of my comfort zone.* Joel forked his eggs and stuffed his mouth, followed by a bite of toast and a swig of coffee.

A man with wavy, auburn hair stood in the doorway...Joel had heard one of the men address him as Mr. Tomas as the men scurried outside. Joel noticed the man appeared bronzed from the sun and tall like a vision of a God statute. He walked over to Joel stared and sat down and began eating.

Later on Lolita said, "Oh, that's Felicite. Don't let him rattle you."

Felicite lifted from the table, cleared his throat, and with hands on his narrow hips, said, "Cotton is being picked today. Care to watch?" Turning he added, "City boy you might want to change clothes, though," and he kept on walking.

She reached over and took his hand. "I'm sure there are jeans around here to fit you, and probably some boots. Come on, I'll help you."

Joel stood, shook off the soft hand, and belted out, "Felicite." He heard the footsteps stop, and Joel said, "Only address me as Dr. Wright. And yes, I'll meet with you later today!" Joel placed his chair under the table and looked into a gaping-mouthed Lolita. "Are you coming with me or not?"

She stood and said, "Let me grab my purse." Not sure where they were going, she hurried and met him on the front porch. He waited by the rental car, opened the passenger door, and closed it behind her. He sat behind the wheel. "Are you familiar with where men's clothing stores might be?"

She smiled widely. "That I am. I think for your style, the Men's Warehouse is where we should try. Take the next right and stay on the road until you see the next county line, and in two or so hours we'll be there."

Joel drove in silence for a while and then asked, "So, tell me, how did my mother know Felix, or how did he come to be the former plantation's foreman?"

Lolita twisted her hands then said, "Joel, pardon my saying so, but it doesn't appear that you know much about your mother." She paused.

"You have me there. My whole life was in boarding school, and only spent a few holidays with my parents. My career path as a doctor was chosen for me, so I am much surprised but pleasantly pleased that I've met you."

"Well, Dr. Wright—"

"You can call me Joel." He turned and smiled.

She returned the smile and said, "Let me begin with some history. Your mother was Creole, according to my grandmother, Carolynn Perce. Your mother's great-great-grandfather, Edward Wright, lived in Europe with his native wife and had a son named Sheppard Wright, who became involved with a female slave. Attorney Sheppard Wright came to New Orleans with child. Your great-grandmother, used her maiden name, Wright. The rest you know."

He placed a hand on her arm and blew out a breath, and thought, *disbelief*, but said, "All right, Lolita, please continue."

According to my mother, your grandmother was cream in color and had gray eyes and blond, curly hair and passed for white. An artist that was passing through did an oil painting of her, and it hangs over the B & B's fireplace. Margaret met another man, also French, and married him. He went back to France and fought in the war against Germany and died in 1940, leaving your grandmother pregnant. She stayed on with Charlotte and my mother at the B. & B…Your grandmother delivered an auburn-haired male child with cobalt-blue eyes and named him Felix, who resembled both his mother and his father. Felix traveled around, but in his twenties, he moved back to New Orleans. However, your mother, Elena, hadn't been adopted, and kept the Wright name." She eyed Joel. "My, I've been talking this whole time."

Joel pulled into the Men's Warehouse lot and said, "We'll table this history talk for now, Lolita, and thank you for sharing. It's a lot to mull over." He opened her door and placed his hand automatically on her back. She shivered, and he felt a tingle travel up his arm. Inside the store, she suggested several outfits and pointed to a pair of boots. He shrugged his shoulders, chuckling, said, "I'll try these on."

He stepped from the dressing room and removed the jeans' tag. "What do you think?" He breathed deeply and began to relax.

"Why, you look debonair, like you belong in the South." She tilted her head back and her brown eyes locked. She bit her lower lip and reached for his other purchases and hurriedly walked to the register.

He stood still for a moment, thinking, *She is so spontaneous, snappy, and lovely like no one I've ever been with or seen.* She snapped her fingers, and, laughing, he whipped out his credit card. In the car, he asked, "Have you ever ridden a horse?"

"I have, and I'm quite good, if I say so myself. I love the air in my face and the sun's warmth on my back."

"Would you care to ride along with me out to the northern cotton field this afternoon?"

"I'd be delighted, and thank you." She sat quiet for a long time then said, "Joel, the son from your grandmother's marriage is your mother's stepbrother. Your mother visited New Orleans often where she reacquainted herself with Felix. On one of her trips, he told her of a rundown plantation in Mississippi that was for sale. They traveled there together, and your mother loved the place so and she bought it, servants and all. She hired Felix as the plantation's foreman and agreed that he be a fourth owner. He was a very private man and chose to build a small house on the property instead of living in the plantation house. Felix worked the fields and married one of the field crop workers. Their product child was Felicite. He followed his father all over the grounds and adored your mother. When she came for a visit to the plantation, she would read to him. She paid for his education abroad, in which Felicite finally majored in horticulture. Joel, he is your first cousin."

Joel blew out a long whistle. "What? Does he know who I am? I mean, besides my title?"

Lolita touched his leg. He almost got whiplash from turning to look at her. His leg felt the warmth where she had touched.

She batted her long black eyelashes and smiled. She answered, "He does. Your mother brought you here only once when you were five years old, and the two of you played together. That was when your mother and Felix decided Felicite would be the next foreman and he would inherit his father's fourth ownership of the plantation. And all this should be recorded in your mother's legal paperwork."

He nodded. "When I received the paperwork, I skimmed over it and began my journey without really reading any details. My bad." Joel drove in silence the rest of the way to the plantation. In his bedroom, Joel pulled out the long document and read. He wanted to be sure, so he called the attorney again. "Mr. Wilk, this is Dr. Wright. My question, is Felicite really a legal part owner to the plantation?"

"Dr. Wright, don't you ever read? On page 202 it outlines his rights. His ownership is in the land and a percentage of the profits it produces. The plantation house, barns, servants is all yours, and your responsibility to maintain and pay for. The plantation is paid off, and your mother set up a trust fund out of the profits that, so far, has paid all the bills. But both you and Felicite must be in agreement if either party wants to sell out, whether it be just the land, or the plantation house, the building, et cetera. Or if you both chose to sell everything, both must be in total agreement."

"What about my uncle, or his wife?"

"Dr. Joel Taylor Wright, the birth and death certificates are in an envelope inside the folder I gave you. But so you know, Felix's wife died during childbirth of her only child, Felicite. Felix never remarried, and had no said child with any other woman. He died in 2009. Here's a brief report on Felicite and his father. They were in the field pulling a newborn calf from the high waters of the creek. It had reportedly rained several inches in a short span. As Felix hosted the animal up to his son, he lost his footing and the maddening current swiftly pulled Felix away. And before Felicite could anchor the calf and reach his father, Felix went under and drowned. Sad story. Joel, Felicite is a good man, a hard worker, and is very well respected in the county. He gives a fair wage for a decent day's work. And Felicite works right alongside with the crop men, women, and their children. You both are a lot alike. Single, hard workers, smart, and wealthy. Joel, stay on the line, I need to take this call."

Joel laid his cell phone on the dresser with speaker on. He hung up his clothes and placed his tie and shoes in the closet. He heard, "You still there?"

"I am. Go ahead, please."

"By now, you probably have observed that most of the plantation staff and field workers are of a different race. Everyone on the plantation is a direct descent from their forefathers, who worked the plantation before the Civil War. Everyone is there of their own free will and is paid an honest wage. All reputable individuals. My advice to you, son, is get to know each of the workers. Sorry, but my other line is ringing again. Good luck, Dr. Joel." The lines silenced.

He sat on the four-poster bed glanced at his watch. The time now was two thirty. He again shook his head in disbelief, and thought, *I have a first cousin, and one I'm not too sure I even like.* He reached for the legal paperwork and opened the envelope.

3

JOEL PUT THE papers away and headed down to the south wing and rapped on Lolita's door.

"Hello, I was just resting." Her robe gaped.

Joel's eyes widened as he glanced down. Her skin looked creamy and soft. He placed his hands in his pockets so as not to reach out and touch her. He asked, "Do you still want to go horseback riding with me to the cotton field?"

She nodded, then said, "I'll be right down. Meet me at the stables," and flashed a bright smile. He took two steps at a time and almost ran to the stable. He barked, "Saddle up two horses, one for me and one for Ms. Lolita"—and then softened his voice—"Thank you." He stood, glancing at the horses and silently marveling how well maintained they were. She touched his back and the hairs on his neck rose. He slowly breathed out and turned with a smile. "Lolita. Our horses are ready to ride."

Thirty-five minutes later, they were watching Felicite with the field hands. Nothing modern was in the field. No shiny equipment or field-watering device; just life in the 1800s. Women wore dresses and aprons and men wore jeans or bibbed overalls. They carried bamboo baskets, which held their pickings. Several children carried water buckets and dippers, stopping at the end of each row for the field hands to take a drink. When the picked cotton filled the baskets, Felicite, muscles bulging, and another man lifted them on a cart pulled by two work horses. Then a driver and a field hand would head the team of horses to the barn. Joel rose in his saddle and watched. The men would exchange the full cart for an empty one and bring it back to the field. And the cycle repeated. It was now five thirty. A bell dinged and quitting time had arrived. The men, women, and children scattered and disappeared within minutes from the field.

Felicite said, "So I see you made it to the cotton field. What's your take on the operation?"

"Well"—scrubbing his face—"Watching the workers took me back in time, before modern machinery was invented. Have you ever thought on modernizing the cotton's production methods?"

"Dr. Wright." He flung his hat against his leg and with his other arm wiped his brow. "We'll talk business later. I must hurry and wash up, or no dinner." He bowed at Lolita and scurried away, muttering in broken French.

Joel glanced over to Lolita. "What?"

She only said, "If you want dinner, you will have to be at the table by six." And she kicked her horse in its sides.

They hurried to the house. Lolita jumped down and went inside. Joel reached for Lolita's horse's reins and rode to the barn. A stable hand and boy reached for the horses' leads. Joel made a quick rush into the house and jaunted upstairs. In his bedroom, he did a nippy wash-up in the basin and in three minutes, shaved, slid into a business suit and tie, and verily graced the stairs. He briskly walked to the dining area and saw the workers, Felicite, and Lolita eating.

Felicite, at the head of the long table, took a drink of iced tea, but glanced up and caught Joel's eye. His deep-blue eyes darted intensity. Lolita made light conversation and gave up with the men. Soon afterward, she made departing excuses and left for her bedroom. The men stood. The field hands left the dining room after nodding to Felicite. Both Joel and Felicite retired to the drawing room for men talk. The servant poured both men an after-dinner drink; Joel downed his while Felicite sipped. The room crackled with silence. Felicite didn't broaden the previous question about bringing modernization to the cotton fields, but did ask, "Dr. Wright, do you intend on selling your proportion of the plantation?"

Joel reached his glass out to the servant again and said, "Sir, I would like a black coffee, and thank you." He glanced at his cousin, matching his stare, and let out a breath. "I don't know! This plantation is a new discovery, as are other things that I'm pondering through."

Felicite nodded. "It's strange seeing you here after all these years. I'm sorry for your loss, mother and father." His brow lifted. "I didn't really know your father, but Mrs. Elena Wright Taylor was a fine woman. She treated me more like a mother than an aunt and I am forever indebted to her."

"Thank you, Felicite, for your words of kindness. I don't recall our meeting in our younger days, but I've heard. And I regret you never knew your mother and for the loss you must feel about your father. I understand he contributed so much to the restoration of the plantation's house, the crop fields, and aided with the improved line of *Hereford* as the specific breed of beef cattle."

Felicite nodded. "It was your mother's leading direction for me to major in horticulture and being under my father's wing that I learnt the land. I love it here." He rose. "I have money, if you decide to sell your portion. After all, you're quite the city man through and through." Chuckling, he added, "And clothes don't make the man."

"Felicite, I don't care to argue. I'm more than sure after I process everything we'll talk. I'm leaving in the morning to take care of my father's unfinished business. Here's my number if you need to reach me. But make no doubt I will return." He unfolded from the chair and, spine straight, said over his shoulder, "Anything happening between you and Ms. Aime?"

Felicite patted his knee and hardily laughed. "A man doesn't kiss and tell."

Joel walked from the room fisting and unfisting his hands. In his bedroom, he packed his suitcase and placed it by the door. His thoughts returned to a certain lady named Ms. Lolita Aime. He couldn't seem to wait until he saw her again. He liked her flare and enjoyed listening to her talk. She was just different, puzzling, and pretty. Joel lay in bed and watched the fan blade go around. Sleep came.

The next morning at breakfast, he nodded to Felicite and said to the other at the table, "Lolita. May I speak with you?" He stood by her chair, waiting for a reply.

Felicite cleared his throat, covering a chuckle.

She sweetly answered, "Of course."

Felicite said, "Lolita, don't forget our meeting in my office." And he left the house.

Joel sat and ate, but the food swelled in his mouth. He downed it with coffee. She stood, and he followed. She waltzed into the drawling room with hands held behind her back, swaying in her bright-blue dress. It swished as she moved; she was magnetizing. He felt warm being near her, as if she had cast a spell on him. He shivered. She turned quickly and they were just inches apart. Her full, red lips were tantalizing. She leaned in, and his senses left him. He pulled her close and bent, kissing her hard, and then softened to the touch. Her lips were sweet to the taste. Joel broke the hold and locked with her mysterious, large brown eyes. He said, "Lolita, I'm sorry. I've acted out of improper character." His breathing was anything but calm. "Do you have a bow? Are you courting anyone? I should have asked you first."

She shook her head. "Why, Dr. Wright?"

He wrapped his arms tighter around her waist and went in for another kiss. Both came up for air, breathing in gasps. He needed to get far from this woman; she was like a legal drug. He squared his shoulders. "Lolita, I'm leaving for Ohio in a little while to care for my father's unfinished business. How long will you be staying on at the plantation?"

"Must you go at this time? I would like for us to get better acquainted and learn about each other's likes and dislikes."

He reached for her hand. "I need to do this. Will you be here when I come back?"

"No, Joel, the first of the week I'm going home to the B. & B...My mother, Lynen, will need help in running the place. It's almost our busiest season coming up. Mother will want to know all the news here and about your parents. If you decide you would care to call on me, come to New Orleans, but don't put off too long." She squeezed his hand and swished from the room.

He stood and could do nothing but stare after her.

By ten thirty he had spoken with the house employment and assured them that he would return, and left Elsa still in charge. He went to the barn and found Felicite. "Are you comfortable running everything as you have in the past, until I return?"

Then he heard a familiar voice. "Oh, Felicite, you devil, where are you?"

Felicite acknowledged Lolita and kissed her hand. "Please take a seat. I'll be right with you. I wouldn't want to keep a beautiful lady waiting."

Felicite walked out of his office with Joel. "Dr. Wright, let there be an understanding between us. I take my homeland very seriously. Always have always will. Have a safe trip!" He walked into his office and closed the door.

Joel turned on his heel as the laughter poured through the door. The hairs on his neck were rising and he wanted to hit something. Joel left the plantation without another word and drove his rental car back to Kentucky. He placed a classical CD in the slot and listened to the music. Somewhere crossing the state line, thoughts of Lolita kept surfacing: *Her beautiful, glowing skin, her brown sparkling eyes, and her red, red lips.* "Was I just caught up in the moment, taken in by another era in time? Could she have been just any sparkling woman at the plantation that caught my eye?" He thumbed the steering wheel, and said, "I've been without female company way too long."

An hour later, he pulled over at a roadside rest area and retrieved the basket of packed food the cook insisted he take. After three pieces of fried chicken, he couldn't believe himself. Joel peeled the orange and enjoyed its sweet taste. He had never eaten like this. He chuckled. She had even packed a quart of iced tea. Then he rested for an hour.

It was midafternoon when he reached Kentucky and stopped at his parents' home. In the driveway he saw an auction sign posted: For Sale, October 20, 2016. He knocked on the door, and Desiree answered. "Sweet Jesus, Joel. I wasn't expecting you until the auction. Come on in out of that wind. Sure enough a snow is blowing in."

He hugged her and said, "Can I get a coffee from you and a night's stay?"

She shuffled her apron and led the way into the kitchen. The house was mostly stripped down to the bare nothings. "Desiree, is there any furniture left?"

"Oh yes, sir. This small table, two chairs, my bed, dresser, a rocking chair, and your bedroom set. In seventeen days, the house will be sold. Rumor is people are interested in left furnishings."

Sipping the coffee, he asked, "Where will you stay?"

"Don't rightly know, Joel. I lost track of my family years ago. I've lived here most of my life."

"Desiree, I now own a plantation in Mississippi—well, mostly own. My point is—would you consider moving to the plantation? You'd have your own room for as long as you live."

"Is there other dark-skinned people like me working there? And a church?"

"Yes to your first question. Most are the offspring of the servants that were bought or born at the plantation. They are Southern through and through. Really polite and nice. Elsa is the housekeeper. There's a cousin of mine living on the land and he's part French and a part owner. Did you know about him or my mother's plantation?" He yawned again. "Sorry. Oh, and church, I don't know anything about churches in Mississippi, but I will inquire and see what fellowships are available and let you know?"

"Joel, why don't you drink your coffee and eat a piece of sweet potato pie? Then get yourself a good night's sleep and we'll talk more in the morning."

"That's a great idea." He yawned and forked another piece of pie into his mouth. He swigged down the coffee, and brought another bite to his mouth, until the last bite was eaten. Joel then carried his plate and cup to the sink. "Sure is good eating. Night, Desiree."

He removed his watch, shoes, and suit clothes down to his briefs, and lay down in bed with the cover pulled up under his chin. Joel slept through the night and was surprised when he heard Desiree's voice at his door. "Mr. Joel. You awake in there."

"I'll be right out." He paused and listened as her steps faded. Joel stood under the hot steaming shower waters for a few minutes. It was nice to have modern. Then he shaved and dressed in his suit. He sat at the kitchen table eating toast and eggs. He asked, "So did you know about the plantation, Desiree?"

"Yes, I knew. And I wasn't for sure about the cousin. But for me to go South, I'm unsure. You knows, Mr. Joel, skin color doesn't bind you."

"Well, I'm turning in the rental car at the airport and then heading on to Ohio. I need to check out my father's apartment and his research information to see if anything in his writings should be turned in at the hospital. You have my cell number—call me. You're more than welcome to visit the plantation and make up your own mind."

"Joel, aren't you going to be here for the auction?"

"Like I said, you have my number." He thanked her and gave Desiree a hefty hug. He left his parent's house once again a little sad. No longer a homey place.

He returned the rental car and caught his flight. It was quick and smooth. Joel retrieved his luggage and his Porsche then stopped at his high-riser for a business change of clothes. He left his less-than-casual clothes in the laundry basket for the housekeeper to attend to. He saw all his father's stacked boxes and noticed the green blinking light on his answering machine. He sat at his desk with pen in hand, and scrubbed his face. Parties and more parties requesting him to attend. And then there was Jewels. One of his favorite hookup people. She was a flight attendant and traveled the world. And when in Columbus, if he were available, they met. Nothing committal. He checked his calendar, but for some reason deleted the call. Lolita came to mind…and her sweet kiss.

Outside his high-riser his driver was waiting. Joel gave him the address and sat back and fixed a hot tea. In a short span, the driver parked and opened Joel's door. "Wait please."

Oliver nodded, closed the door, and slid behind the wheel of the car and waited.

Joel fiddled with the apartment key and, finally, the door opened. Joel walked into a fully equipped setup. Mostly rustic furniture; another surprise about his father. His desk with computer sat on the left under a pass-through window to the kitchen. He picked up stacks of open paid bills, junk mail, and a sealed envelope address to Dr. Charles Taylor written in a woman's penmanship. He didn't take time to properly open the letter. A picture of a woman and his father fell out. He knelt as the air was sucked out of him. She appeared to be biracial. He made himself read the two pages.

Dr. Wright, my Charles.

I'm sorry things ended last month so abruptly between us. When we began our time together I never expect our relationship to grow or for you to be so kind and understanding. I knew exactly what I was to be: a companion, and an outlet. I understood your wife's situation and the advice you were given in not having any more children because of her weak heart. And there was no doubt that you were devoted and that you love her very much. Our seventeen years together was special, enlightening, and educational. I enjoyed the art shows, music atmosphere, and the theater, but mostly just being here with you and hearing about your research and its trials and errors. You never treated me with any less respect because I was different than you, in color, nationality, and in education. I enjoyed our times together. However, when we were dining at Millie's Restaurant and your old buddy's son walked in and joined our table, I was surprised when you asked him to take me home. It was as if you knew he and I would be instantly attracted to one another. We later talked about this. You gave me your blessing about Tony and our marriage, and explained that your needs in life had changed, stating your age now played a major factor that stood between us and how it was time you learned to live with Elena and place her first in your aging life. Charles, I again thank you for our time and what you've taught me about life.

Your blessing forever, Roseletta.

"My father had an affair! He knew about my mother's weak heart and I didn't, and I'm the heart specialist." He went to the liquor cabinet and poured him a whiskey, and considered another but dumped the bottle. "I wonder if mother knew about his affair." He checked out the apartment's bedroom and no traces were left behind of another person; not even a toothbrush. Other than the furnishings, it appeared to be a place his father used only for his research purposes. Joel packed up his father's clothes and gathered his personal belongings and set them at the door. He sat down in his father's chair and slid the CD (given to him by the attorney) in the computer slot and watched and listened in disbelief. His father had left a journal about his heritage pedigree. Joel blew out a held breath. His great-great-grandfather was Dr. Zachary Taylor and he married a Bethany William from Boston, from one of the finest diplomatic and influential political families. He was given a hefty amount of money from her father, Senator Benjamin William, for their marriage union. She was married to Dr. Zachary in name only and lived the part of lady of the house to the public, but Zachary's comfort came from a slave woman, and two years later a son was born of that unification and raised as Bethany and his child. The child was named William Taylor. His eyes were as blue as the ocean and his body was milky white. He became a family doctor and settled in Kentucky with a Jenifer Clark, a German girl, who was a friend of the family's. He owned a farm and raised cattle. His wife became ill, and death was in their near future. He found comfort with a slave girl, and a male toadheaded child with gray eyes and light skin was born and handed over to William at birth and raised as Jenifer and his child.

After the death of Dr. William Taylor's wife, the nanny—the birth mother—moved into the house and cared for the master's child, Lloyd Taylor, Joel's grandfather. Joel lowered his head on the corner of his father's desk. His body ached and his mind was buzzing, yet somehow he felt hunger. He removed the CD from the computer placed it in its sleeve with the letter inside his jacket pocket and carried his father's belongings, leaving the apartment.

4

His DRIVER OPENED the trunk and placed the boxes in. He opened the car door for Joel. "Where to, Dr. Wright?"

"Just drive please." Several hours passed before Joel spoke. "Pull in over there." It was a Wendy's. Joel said, "Drop off those boxes to the Goodwill, but take me home first." At the high-riser he paced back and forth, pondering what he was to do next. He couldn't shake the new information from the letter of the acquired family's history. His head pounded. Joel showered and went to bed, promising he would view and listen to the CD tomorrow. But sleep was torturous. Joel tossed and turned and woke in a sweat. He couldn't get past his forefathers' infidelities nor his mother's history. "I've been baptized in the church, taught union, separation, forsaking all others—somehow I felt violated."

Joel prepared a pot of strong coffee and made wheat toast; then he powered up his computer. He placed the CD in the slot and reviewed the generation of men and their results. "Man, from my great-great-grandfather through and including my father, they all had affairs, and all but my father had children as a result." He considered this knowledge and thought on his mother's side of the family and their contribution to his heritage. According to Lolita Aime, his mother's mother, his grandmother, was Margaret Wright of Creole descent. And she had an Indian brave's baby girl child; his mother, Elena Wright, was both Creole and Blackfeet

Indian with a dash of white. She married Charles Taylor, and they birthed a blue-eyed blond son named Joel Taylor Wright. His name was insisted on by his mother, Elena Wright Taylor, so the Wright name would be carried out. Joel sat staring and began to laugh and said, "Counting my heritage from my father's side I'm a ten-nation, all-in-one kind of a guy. If I don't laugh I'll cry." He powered down the computer, filed the CD, and shuffled though the boxes of his father's research work, file after file.

Several hours had passed. Joel was sweaty, dirty with printed ink marks, and furious from being excluded as a family member to his mother and father. Oh, he had been groomed right and given benefits that most children never receive, but hiding one's nationality and assumed under another identity somehow just wasn't right. He had mixed emotions boiling and they were about to explode. All the generations on both sides of the family had hidden secrets. For what purpose? His head ached and his body was sore. He still kept thinking, *How many other people's five generations would be similar?* He shuffled through his father's work and found update information that could make a breakthrough in aiding many people with headaches. He called the hospital and reported the breaking news to his father's work partner. There was a clap of hands in the background, and Joel silently smiled. He ended the call and rang for his driver. Joel felt his life spinning out of control. His driver loaded the car and waited.

After a brisk hot shower, a shave, and dressed in business attire he was ready to face the world. At the hospital, he was greeted royally, and everyone at once spoke. He laughed. This was his world, his element. The boxes were dropped off and the research staff began studying his father's work. Joel checked in with his staff and consulted them about several patients, then left for his high raiser. He ordered in and read from the diary. It coincided with his father's CD. Joel's head ached. His mind was stretched and an unfamiliar loneliness surrounded him. If only there was someone to speak with; a living soul to share his thoughts. He searched through the aged trunk and saw the childhood clothing and a gold cross. Joel, on bended knee, wept. He didn't know how long he was there, but the tears stopped and the heaviness was gone. Joel needed to man up and face the responsibility of his parents' house. After all, he was business-minded. He made personal arrangements to trade in his Porsche and purchase an orange Toyota Tundra with four doors, and still he made money. His mind was made up; he was keeping the plantation, but Joel knew definitely he would make some modern updates.

He called Desiree. "I'm driving and should reach the house in five hours. I'd appreciate dinner when I arrive, if that's not too much trouble."

"Joels, you know there's no trouble getting you fed. Now drive sensibly."

He chuckled. *She's always the same.* He gathered most of his belongings and had his king-sized bed, bedding, dresser, mirror, two nightstands, and lamps shipped to the plantation. Joel packed all his clothes, personal toiletries, jewelry, and the treasured trunk and placed them in the covered truck's bed. Joel listed his high-riser with a renowned realtor and let the manager of the building know of his move. Joel called his driver and gave a nice severance package, and they shook hands. Joel hoisted up in his truck, tapped the steering wheel, and prayed, "Guide me and give me wisdom in my life and with work, in love and in my community, and the strength to deal with Felicite."

At his parent's house, he and Desiree ate and enjoyed their conversation. Late into the night, they were reminiscing of his youth, his father's research, and his mother's love for music. Nothing was mentioned or even acknowledged about his father's mistress. He doubted Desiree knew. He rolled into bed and for the first time in a long while, he slept sound. The next morning, breakfast was ready and waiting. Joel, still in business suit, addressed Desiree, "Well, have you thought over visiting the plantation?"

"Joels, I have, but I'm too old to change my lifestyle. I've done some calling around and found a distant cousin who I can live with, and the strangest part is Madelyn lives only three streets over. She has twin boys and works for the state. I would be their nanny. I'm to meet with her and the boys next week."

"I can take you over to Madelyn's house so you don't have to walk. I'll wait for you outside."

"I'd like that, Joels. I saw your new truck, orange and pretty. Better than that low-down-to-the-curb car you drove.

"Thank you. Desiree, if you change your mind staying on with your cousin, make a phone call, and I'll personally come bring you to the plantation." Joel impulsively hugged Desiree and kissed her black cheek. She swatted at him and hugged him back.

Later in the day, Joel asked Desiree, "What do you know about Felicite?"

"Now, now, don't scowl. You knows your momma loved you, but that father of yours was very military mannered with you. That's why she loved visiting the plantation. She felt free and relaxed. Ms. Elena thought the Southern air did her good. Your father only allowed her to take you once to the plantation. When you came back that summer you acted like a child, not a mime of him. Your mother enjoyed Felicite's childish charm and the way he hung on to each word she read or just holding him on her lap. Things she didn't get to enjoy with you. She realized, as Felicite grew, he had a real love for the land and the care he gave it, so she sent him abroad with his father's permission and paid for Felicite's education. Horticulture was his major. Your mother tried to play matchmaker with her New Orleans friend's daughter, but your mother passed before anything of value materialized. Joel, he's a good, honest man." She sniggered. "Have you ever really looked in the mirror? Yous and him are same height, build, the same attitude, and character. All but yours hair and eye color are different. He's a doctor of the land and you a doctor of the heart. Lands almighty."

Joel flexed his fisted hands and then relaxed, thinking. He and his mother never got to be close, and poor Felicite never got to know his mother. They were both cheated, educated, and were passionate about their career, and maybe interested in the same woman. Well, they were more alike than he wanted to admit. Lolita came to mind. *What had Felicite wanted in seeing her before I left?* Then the laughter. Were they making fun of him, the northerner?

The next several hours Joel spent on the phone talking with Mississippi's Hospital Benefits Department. After a back-and-forth conversation and an agreement, Joel was much more settled. He heard Desiree's steps and opened his bedroom door. "Yes?"

"Dinner is being taken out the oven."

"I'll be right down after I shower and shave. Thank you." He closed the door and just breathed. He was once again in what was his parents' house. Joel selected his business attire to wear to dinner for this was his training since a child. Thirty minutes later, he carried in his used clothes and asked, "Desiree, do the dry cleaner's still do pick-up and delivery?"

"Put your things in the laundry chair and I'll see to them. Now set down and eat!"

He smiled, his dimple deepening, and obeyed. That's night sleep was restless. He tossed and turned, plumped the pillows, threw off the covers, and lay with his hands behind his head, thinking, *I've acted like my father, quick to judge Felicite. Now there's a wall between us, and I'll be moving there soon. After all, a man has his pride.* He padded to the kitchen and poured a glass of iced water and drank. Back in his bed, sleep came, until he saw Lolita's face and her smiling brown eyes. He bolted upright. *Only a dream.* He would make a point to ask Desiree if she knew or had information on the mysterious woman, Lolita. He rushed down to breakfast and enjoyed the eggs, bacon, fried potatoes, and toast. The strong coffee was a delight.

After breakfast, Desiree left for the market, and Joel called the apartment complex where his father had studied. It was confirmed that his father owned the unit. The manager of the complex was only too happy to find a buyer and one that would take it furnished. Joel agreed to pay for a cleaning staff to air out and wash walls and whatever else was needed to make the property available for purchase. Joel gave the manager the attorney's name and firm address for his check from the sale of the apartment to be forwarded to. He breathed easier. The afternoon had passed and evening was on the horizon. The doorbell rang, and Joel answered. His dry cleaning was returned. He tipped the driver. After placing his clothing away, he heard that familiar old voice, "Joels, it's dinner time."

He shuffled to the kitchen and ate. Joel helped clear the table and offered to dry dishes. She batted him away with her apron. "Lands of mercy, set and I'll bring you an iced tea."

He chuckled and sat. A few minutes later, he approached the subject of Lolita. "Tell me what you know about the woman." He watched her head shake. Then she turned and took a chair across from him. "Your mother'd enjoyed going to New Orleans once a year. She loved the thrill of the Mardi Gras, the ball, the parade, and the festival events. How she would light up when her friend called. Although your momma mostly watched from a distance, but sometimes her brother would escort her to the events. They had a fun, adoring connection. When Lolita was born, she and your mother became close. By then, Ms. Elena's brother had moved to the plantation and had his son Felicite. Lolita became your mother's young companion. When she turned seventeen, your mother paid for Lolita to leave New Orleans and travel and go to school in Paris. Lolita wrote weekly to your mother. Sometimes she would read to me and she would almost burst with pride. She helped Lolita escape wrong romances and was stern with her. Lolita's relation, Carolynn Perce, was much too busy in keeping the B & B afloat to look after the welfare of their granddaughter as her mother, and they gave full permission to Ms. Elena. When Lolita graduated and returned home, Ms.

Elena had her accompany them to the plantation. She was introduced to Felicite and they talked, took walks, and did some horseback riding, but their last trip was cut short. Your mother had a breathing issue and they returned home—Lolita to New Orleans and your mother to Kentucky. Her husband doted on her, and for a while she seemed stronger, but your father died and your mother couldn't keep up her strength. Ms. Elena so wanted to travel one last time to New Orleans. She was hopeful of saying words of encouragement to bring Felicite and Lolita together. Both dated others, but your mother wanted a joined union. Something about anchoring the plantation's future."

"Desiree, do you think Felicite and Lolita have that romantic bond?"

"What's your interest, Joels? Are you just wanting to make her a trophy to yous or are yous genuinely interested? Question ask yous before making the wrong decision." She lifted from the chair and rubbed her back. "Too much sitting." She muttered, "There's been decades of wrongness." She shuffled to her bedroom. "Night, Joels."

He felt uncertain. How much did Desiree know about his family history? "Night, Desiree." Joel went into his bedroom and let his clothes drop on the floor, headed for the shower. The waters cascaded over his body until he felt refreshed. Joel slipped into bed, and that night sleep came.

A week slipped by before Desiree met with her family and they instantly bonded. She was so excited and younger-appearing. She rattled all the three blocks home. Joel thought, *Those twins will be so loved and well cared for*. He had been by his nanny. He let out an audible sigh. As a grown man, he squared his shoulders and was once again ready to face life head-on.

In the house, he dressed in business attire, for within fifteen minutes the auction sale of his parents' house would begin. Joel greeted people, shook hands, and answered every property question.

He glanced in Desiree's direction. She had done her usual, baking dozens of cookies. He smiled and was sure that her variety of cookies had driven up the sale. A lovely couple with a boy child and girl child yelled when they found out they had outbid the crowd. They approached Desiree and asked, "Would you stay on as our housekeeper, cook, and nanny? We'll double your wages?"

Desiree fluffed her apron and said, "Mrs. Dalton, I's now have Friday afternoon through Sunday evening off with pay, and I am given a two-weeks paid vacation and holidays, even if I's am not needed, and this includes my room and board. Just so yous don't misunderstand, meal time is when I says so."

Mrs. Dalton and her husband, Gary, agreed and handed Desiree her first paycheck, although they were a month out from moving in. Desiree cornered Joel, and he drove her to the cousin's house and explained she wouldn't be moving in with her after all, but thanks for the welcome. They both agreed they had each other and would visit, not letting family slip back through the cracks.

Joel stayed at the house of the new owners-to-be for another three days, and found suddenly he felt relaxed. He once again placed the CD in his computer's slot and was as shocked, watching and listening to it, as the first time. Joel said, "The men in my family have been dishonest and deceiving about their heritage and their personal life." He went for a walk and questioned, "How do I perceive myself? Do I go forward and ignore the heritage knowledge, or do I confess that I'm a ten-nation being, or do I stay true to myself? And what about if I should meet my soul mate—do I come clean and honest?" Joel laughed, "Soul mate!" The next morning, he was carrying his tote bag to the truck.

Desiree said, "Joels, there's things you can learn about your momma and your grandmamma in New Orleans at the B & B. Both were splendid ladies." She kissed him on his white cheek and squeezed him in a long hug. "Keep in touch with your ole nanny."

Promises were made. Joel placed his tote in the truck and swung up behind the wheel. He thought, *Should I drive to the plantation and talk with Felicite? Hopefully we can come to an understanding, and maybe I will apologize for my Northern behavior. Or should I drive to New Orleans and learn more about my grandmother and my mother's heritage?* He started the engine and drove, but hot Lolita came to his mind. An hour and a half later down the road, he made a sharp turn and headed his truck to New Orleans. The trip would take approximately twenty-two hours straight through, but after six grueling hours and orange barrels with so many delays, he found a motel and spent the night. "Tomorrow is another day." He switched the lights off in the motel, plumped his pillow, and hoped to sleep.

5

LOLITA SAT AND sipped on an iced tea, thinking over her offer to Felicite. He had laughed, but it appeared friendly. Would he really seek after her dream and find an Appaloosa colt, bred from a black Friesian line and an American Appaloosa? Would he then board the horse at the plantation and aid her in training the horse? Despite her not wanting to leave the plantation, she needed to return to the B & B and help encourage her mother to hire more help. She would address the horse subject again later with Felicite. Lolita stayed a few more days, and then left on Monday as promised to Joel.

Felicite offered to drive her to New Orleans, and she accepted. The drive was over three hours and forty-five minutes long, due to her insisting they stop and eat and just not rush. Again she brushed the subject of the colt and Felicite said, "Why not. You know there's a monthly fee for boarding, but I won't charge you in finding the perfect breed or in the training of him."

"Oh, Felicite, you are quite the man. How much is the boarding fee?"

He chuckled and said, "Let's wait until I find an Appaloosa, then we'll talk."

She nodded and smiled.

In his reliable beat-up truck, she touched his forearm and asked, "What's your take on your cousin?"

His facial appearances changed and his chiseled jaw firmed. His nose flared, and his flirty eyes grew cold. But he said, "Lolita, Dr. Joel Taylor Wright is a much respected, educated man, wealthy as I, and noncommittal to a woman—that is, so far." Then he smiled and it widened, reaching his eyes. "Watch yourself, Lolita, and guard your heart. Men like our breed have seen too much, know too much, and we love the women, but we do not fall in love with them." He eyed her face.

"Felicite, I heard what you said, but why haven't you married, really? You're a great catch. Debonair, handsome, funny, charming, well groomed, hardworking—and money doesn't hurt." She turned so she could face him.

"My sweet chérie, working the plantation's land is hard work, and it has been my mistress, but what's to say should I meet the right woman. If one even exists."

The rest of the ride was enjoyable as they bantered back and forth and listened and sometimes sung to a song playing on the truck's radio. Felicite came to the B & B and swung her mother around. She pounded at his hard chest and squealed. He just laughed. A time of speaking with one another was taken as well as a briefing of the newest co-owner of the plantation, whom they called Mr. Northerner. They viewed the overhead portrait of Joel's grandmother, Margaret Wright, and discussed how he was a carbon copy of her, except that he had lighter skin, but their eyes and their hair color were the same. Then Felicite said, "I can even see myself in her. Not the coloring so much, but the bone structure. I guess my cousin and I do look more like each other than either of us is comfortable to admit." He spent the night and headed back to the plantation the next morning.

At the B & B, life was busy with all the people comings and goings. Lolita's mother had hired a full-time cook, which certainly helped, but Lolita suggested they hire a full-time housekeeper and a maid. She had changed thirty-two beds and the laundry was ongoing. The twelve bathrooms were finally cleaned for the day and work would begin all over again in a few short hours. Just like the day before. Lolita paused and glanced at the oil portrait that hung for years over the fireplace. "Small world. Felicite and Joel are first cousins." She shook her head and carried the mop water to the basement and dumped it in the floor drain. Lolita was tired and her body ached; she moved her head from shoulder to shoulder. Walking the steps again, she found her mother and said, "Goodnight, I'm going to turn in for the night."

Her mother blew a kiss.

After her long, floral bubble bath, Lolita polished her toenails red, red. She sat on the edge of her bed, and flashbacks of Dr. Joel Taylor Wright confused her. Had Joel wanted her to stay on at the plantation? Was he interested in her as a woman? Had their kiss meant anything, or was he a tease? Her head spun. One thing was for sure; she was going to get a grip on her emotions and shake herself free of the Northerner, that Dr. Joel Taylor Wright. She swooned, "Even if he is handsome, well built, with thick blond hair and has those dazzling blue eyes." A giggled slipped.

Two weeks passed, and Lynen, Lolita's mother, showed her a written list of to–dos, including the needs for the B & B. Her mother confessed, "I would like to supervise and let someone else do all the work from now on…What do you want out of life, Lolita?"

Her thoughts immediately shifted to the broad-shouldered doctor, but Lolita said, "I asked Felicite to find me an Appaloosa colt and he has agreed to board him and see to his training. I'm not sure what I want out of life, but the B & B is not where I always want to be." She reached out for her mother's hand. "Mother, you've built a well-respected establishment, and business is flourishing. The place is modern, yet you've done a marvelous job of blending in the old with the new. I'm proud of you." They hugged. Lolita said, "I know life hasn't been easy for you here with me, but I love you so, Mother." She kissed her forehead and stepped outside for a walk. Glancing at the smoke-filled skies, she asked herself, "Why am I so unsettled? I wish I could get a glimpse of the bright shining stars, but the New Orleans fireworks in the distance cause cloud coverage." She suddenly hungered for the majestic firmament at the plantation. She sighed. "The air there is so fresh to breathe." Reluctantly, she went inside and spent another restless night.

The next day, the painters showed up at the B & B, and her mother was speaking in Spanish to the workers. "White on house, the wood shutters a soft gray, and the front door in vivid red." Her hands were on her hips as she went inside the B & B. She spoke with Lolita and had her sign in the new boarders and the leaving boarders. Dinnertime was announced and the guests were served. Everyone gave praise to the new chef. He was awesome and cooked traditional jambalaya and gumbo as well as great classic Creole dishes, po-boy and red beans with rice, capturing the bold Cajun flavors. The evening hour passed and the guests went on about the town, knowing the lockdown time at the B & B. The overhead door dinged, and Lolita looked over at her mother. "Expecting anyone this late?"

"No." She shrugged her narrow shoulders.

"You need my help for anything?"

"No, Lolita, you go on and head up for bed. See you in the morning. Night, love." Lynen went to the door, expecting a drop-in boarder for the night. Her mouth gaped, then she said, blocking the doorway, "Well, well, if it isn't that Dr. Northerner. What brings you here?"

"Excuse me, did I need to call in advance to book a room?" He sat his overnight bag down and reached out his hand, then moved it back to his side. "Ms. Lynen Aime, I'm Elena Taylor Wright's son."

"I know who you are, but what are you doing sniffing around here?"

"May I come in?"

She didn't budge.

"Ma'am, I met Ms. Lolita Aime at the plantation, and she spoke of my grandmother and that her portrait hangs over the fireplace here at the B & B. I would like to see for myself and learn more about my heritage. I'm sorry if in some way I have offended you." His mystical blue eyes locked with her piercing brown ones.

She pursed her lips then said, "Bring your bag and we'll register you for the night." Lynen moved aside and led the way to the counter.

He signed in as Dr. Joel Taylor Wright and handed her his visa. She made a copy for the charges and handed his key over. Lynen escorted him to the stairway and said, "Third room on the right. A light meal will be sent to your room. If you need anything else tonight, use the house phone and push in 13, which registers your room. Someone will answer. Breakfast is served promptly at 6:00 a.m."

He smiled and nodded, then squared his shoulders and walked the stairs like it was a plank on a ship. Inside the room, he let out a held breath, and found the space to be quite spacious, although the room was a little dark for his liking and the furniture was more to his mother's taste. In the middle of the room was a marble-canopy four-poster bed made up in red and gold bedding. The matching engraved nightstand held a lit pillared lamp. The massive matching dresser had a framed square mirror resting on it. A high-back mohair sofa sat on the other side of the room where a huge pedestal table and a gold, velvet chair was clustered. The draperies were clean but bulky, old, and red. The closet was narrow and could hardly hold his clothing and shoes. He walked into the bathroom suite and almost cried. A toilet stared at him, and there was a wide sink. He noticed the claw-foot tub and, to his surprise, a shower. Joel sat, untied his shoes, slipped off his silk socks, and wiggled his toes. Next, he stripped off his business attire and showered. A towel was wrapped around his waist when a rap came on his door. He slightly opened the door, but no one was there. A tray sat on a pull-out stand holding a sandwich, potato wedges, and an iced tea. He carried the tray into the room balanced on one hand, with the other hand clutching the towel. Joel sat at the table and prayed. That night, sleep came, and he missed breakfast the next morning. He found a portable one-cup coffeemaker and was delighted coffee packets were included. Joel lifted his cell phone and call Felicite.

"Hello. Who is this?"

"Don't hang up. It's your cousin, Joel."

An audible sigh escaped.

"Felicite, I'm calling to inform you that I'm moving into the plantation house. I arranged my furniture and belongings to be sent, and they may arrive before me."

"So is this a permanent move or is your stay to size up the place before putting it up for sale, Dr. Wright?" Felicite huffed.

Joel said, in almost a whisper, "Felicite, I owe you an apology. My behavior and manners have been rude. I trust we can talk, and perhaps in time become friends. I'll be at the plantation in a few days. Think over what I've said." Joel sat for a long time holding a silent cell phone. He wished he had a Bible to research his question on humbleness. "That was something not taught in my parents' house, except by Desiree, and she also has a natural, genuine kind flare, and so did Lolita. I've been a jerk."

Joel continued making phone calls and going about family business until later that night. He prepared for bed and opened the nightstand top drawer, and there lay a Bible. He opened to James chapter 4 and read verse 10: *Humble yourselves before the Lord, and He will lift you up.* Joel felt he should submit to this higher power and speak to Him directly. He ended up saying, "Show me meekness and offer me gentleness to share with others as You have and do. Give me undeserving mercy and grace." He rose from his knees lighter and realized all of his training, as in his father's military training, was mostly one-sided. Joel quietly slipped on his slacks and went to his truck, searching through the trunk, and found the childhood cross his mother had given him as a boy. He bowed his head and realized there was a deeper depth to Elena Wright Taylor than he had known. One of great cost was her submission to his father. On the tailgate, he cried for the lost past, the missed opportunities with his mother, and the just-now awakening in faith. Joel retired to the bedroom suite and lay down, vowing to be a better spiritual and physical person with God's lead; but still sleep evaded him. The next morning, Joel sat at the breakfast table. Twenty or so other guests had gathered and some were chattering. The meal was served, round table. The coffee was poured into the cups and OJ was offered. Everyone seemed to enjoy the hearty breakfast. As the breakfast guests left one by one, he found himself wandering into the parlor. With hands behind his back, he stared at the oil portrait of his grandmother, Margaret Wright. She was a breathtakingly beautiful woman. Her Creole skin glowed and her long tendrils of blond hair accented her face. Her magnetic blue eyes gave the impression that they were following you. He was surprised at how much he and his mother resembled her.

"Joel?"

He turned and faced Lolita. "Hello."

"When did you arrive?"

"Last night."

"Why are you here?" she asked sweetly.

"I've come to find out more about my heritage."

Lolita pouted, then said, "I thought you, um, well, never mind."

"I need your help, Lolita. Your mother appears angry with me, and I don't know why. I wish to talk with her, for she was my mother's best friend and the B & B. is where my parents met."

Lolita slowly smiled and said, "I'll talk with my mother and see if she will speak with you."

"Thank you." He turned and walked from the room.

Lolita shivered, but this time she was left cold. She wanted to hit something or sputter some unkind words in Spanish. Her heart ached for the man. She immediately went searching for her mother. After the evening meal, Lynen leaned over Joel's chair. "Care to join me in the parlor?"

He lifted from his chair and followed her, with Lolita close on his heels. Her mother's eyes darted around him and she said, "Lolita, leave and close the drawing doors behind you."

"But, mother."

"Now. What I have to say is for his ears only."

Joel stood with legs apart and hands in his slacks pockets firmly. He listened as Lolita's steps faded and said, "Ms. Aime, thank you for seeing me."

"Dr. Joel Taylor Wright, I'd ask you to sit, but you won't be in here that long." A chill aired the room. "When I'm finished, please leave the B & B. and don't ever come back."

His eyebrows arched, but he kept silent. He shifted his weight and placed his hands behind his back. Lynen's dark brown eyes were almost black and her English was heavily accented. "You've heard the old saying that the apple doesn't fall far from the tree?"

He stared intently and nodded.

"Your mother was a saint in my book! Let me begin, your grandmother Margaret Wright was proud that her daughter was French, Indian, and a Caucasian mix. The fact that Margaret was a squaw didn't hold well in the white folks' community, but in New Orleans people are curious, closed-mouthed, and eventually accept you for yourself. Margaret worked hard washing and ironing for other people so she could send her daughter, your mother, abroad to Paris, where Elena could study the arts and music. Your mother was an excellent student and could have gone far, but her mother fell ill and Elena gave up on her dream and came home. She cared for her. Margaret died two weeks later.

"Your mother was about to turn eighteen. Then that pompous man, now your father, had to take Captain Tomas up on his offer and stay at the B & B." Lynen gritted her teeth. "Oh, in the beginning when Elena and Dr. Lt. Charles met, they seemed awesome. He doted after her and used his charms and ways and he cast a spell on her. She loved that man…Their lives read of bliss, and a whirlwind marriage was planned. Society called it romantic. I called it a tragedy. Elena could see no wrong in Charles, and to her he could do no wrong. She worshiped that man. Soon after marriage, she became pregnant and became weakened, requiring a lot of bed rest. Your mother contacted me, and I came to Kentucky with Desiree, and we cared for her. Your father changed in his stature and personality when he found out about your mother's heritage. His whole life had been planned around politics. Your mother, to his upbringing and society, had come from a shameful background, and he couldn't afford a political setback, so Charles chose a different position in life and became a professor in brain research. He verbalized to your mother that she wasn't graced socially enough and he also frowned on her art and music educational degrees." Lynen poked the log in the fireplace, continuing, "They didn't share any of the same values or political views, and he never agreed with her on her religious beliefs. Dr. Charles was a bitter old man before he was really aged. He was hopping angry when she had you baptized in a quaint church right here in New Orleans." She walked over to the portrait of Margaret Wright and said, "Your mother made excuse after excuse for that arrogant snob of a man, her husband. And after you had been sent away to military boarding school, she busied herself in her music and art world. People loved hearing her play. She made the ivory sing…Elena always mentioned she'd received her talents from her musical mother and that Dr. Charles would smile and applaud in mixed company, but his facial features told the truth, a real hardness. Charles saw his wife was highly kept in clothing and food, and would attend with her in public as needed. He stayed at an apartment for days, years even, calling his absence in the home as due to intense study of the brain patterns. Your mother came to New Orleans as often as she could, and we stayed in touch continually. Elena turned her head against the gossip of her husband and came to his aid often. You better set after all. You look a little pale, if that's possible."

Lynen rang for iced tea for two. "While she was here, she got reacquainted with her stepbrother, Felix. She began to laugh again and seemed stronger. She was so happy when making the purchase of the plantation. It was a resort to her. Elena insisted they have horses, and Felix bought a few riders just for him and her. Elena found a little humble church in Mississippi and would play for them when she was at the plantation. Then my daughter Lolita came along and your mother came to New Orleans to care for us. She made a promised to see that Lolita was as educated in the arts and music as she." Lynen took several sips, and eyed Joel. "Your mother loved life. She believed in people without any reservation, and she prospered greatly in her art and delighted in their displays." Lynen stared at the oil painting then said, "Right before your mother's death, she retrieved your father's safety box from the bank. The bank was due to be demolished, and they had called her, for Dr. Charles had not replied to any of their requests in removing the items. Elena called me. She discovered Charles's great-grandfather's diary and was ever so relieved your genes took after hers and her mother's. Blond, blue-eyed, et cetera. She implied that she mailed the aged diary to you. She carried on about a tingle in her right arm and an achy feeling coming and going in her chest. I advised her to see the doctor or go to the hospital, but your mother just dismissed my words and made arrangement to come out to New Orleans, but we know how that turned out. I'm sorry. I loved Elena and her good spirit."

Joel cleared his throat. "Ms. Aime, I want to thank you for being there for my mother."

Lynen placed a halting hand on his shoulder. "Lolita doesn't know any of the details of the diary, only the whirlwind so-called love story of your parents' meeting and marriage, and I don't intent on her hearing. Understand?"

"Yes, ma'am. I…"

"Dr. Joel Taylor Wright, you're a chip off the wrong block. Your mannerism is conceited and rude. You've come into my home all high and mighty, smug, with a better-than-thou attitude just like your late father. You may have your mother's genes in looks, but your egoistic self comes from only one person, your father. Dr. Northerner, get your bag and hightail it out of the B & B now. You're not welcome here!"

Joel softly walked from the room, packed, and tossed his bag in the back of his truck. He sat behind the wheel in a daze. So much knowledge had been thrown at him—and to be warned that he was a lot like his father. Joel hadn't ever cheated with another woman, and had been upfront with each one that there would be nothing lasting. He had become calloused when it came to affairs of the heart. Joel prided himself that he had worked hard to advance as a doctor. He had made a name and deservingly, so far; he was driven and became the best of the best when it came to the field of cardiology. He heard pecking on his window and saw Lolita. He started the truck's engine, let his window down some, and yelled, "What?"

"Why are you leaving, we didn't get to spend time together." On tiptoe she asked, "Joel, was I just a moment of Northerner pleasure at the plantation?"

Joel glanced up and saw Lolita's mother standing in the B & B's doorway. He momentarily looked down and shivered. Lolita stole his breath away. She was lovely and spirited, and he realized that if he didn't move right then he would haul out of the truck and take her into his arms. He said, "Move out of the way." Joel swerved and barreled from the driveway, causing dust to fly.

Lynen came and joined her crying daughter. "What did he say?" She smoothed Lolita's hair from her face and kissed it.

Hiccupping, she said, "It's what he didn't say." Lolita tilted her head and began walking away. She knew she had fallen for the Northerner, hook, line, and sinker... ***

6

Joel realized he was driving like a mad, demon-possessed man. He slowed down to seventy miles an hour and in record time drove to the plantation. After putting his truck into park his eyes roamed as far as they could see. Joel suddenly realized that he had come to the plantation because it had belonged to his mother. And he desperately just wanted to belong somewhere. He hit the steering wheel with his hand. "I haven't thought this out. If only I had read the will all the way through, I might have known about my parents' heritage." He shook his head. "I'm so ridiculous and egotistical, and I'm just full of myself, you arrogant butt." Joel reached the shifter to reverse while looking backward, and asked, "Where am I to go?" He left the shifter in park and lowered his head and wept, "Why hadn't I ever questioned my father on his religious views or his take on politics, or about our home life? And most of all, why didn't I take time to really know and understand my mother?" Joel turned off the truck's engine and opened the truck door and slid down. He paced back and forth on the dirt drive, muttering to himself, "I only saw myself as a white boy trying to prove that I was better than anyone, including my colleagues. I established an unquestionable reputation in my life, work ethics, and in return I gained power, wealth, and nobility." He kicked at the ground. "Those actions weren't wrong, but now I've discovered that I'm not exactly white, so does this change how society will view me as a person or even a doctor? And now unexpectedly I'm without family or ties, but oh, there's education!" Joel sat on the ground. "What was I thinking? On a whim, I sold the high-riser and gave up my city living for what—a change, in another state, in a place that's way too dated. And accepted a lead position at the state's hospital in Mississippi, in my field, cardiology. And why, because of my fame as a doctor and in my heritage name, the son of the well-known Dr. Charles Taylor and his established wife of the arts, Elena Wright Taylor, with her contributions in fundraising in the state, Mississippi, ha."

A honking noise persisted. He saw it was Felicite driving up in his old beat-up Chevrolet truck, waving. Joel lifted and again huffed and kicked at the dirt. Joel dusted off his business attire and squirmed; he was out of his element and low in spirit. Felicite's smile deepened and a hand went around Joel's shoulder. "Hey, Dr. Northerner, what's got you so down in the mouth?"

Joel didn't dare speak; he might fly into a rage or just burst out crying. His emotions were raw and all over the place. They bounced from love, hate, loneliness, despair, anger, and emptiness, all in a split second, and were new and unsettling.

Felicite said, "We need to clear the drive. Let's go up to the barn."

Joel nodded and swung up into his truck, started the engine, and automatically drove in front of the main barn and parked. Felicite said, "Your shipped things arrived yesterday, and I had Elsa, our in-charge housekeeper, place them in the suite you occupied when you first came. I hope that's all right."

Nodding he said, "Thanks, Felicite. That's more than I deserve."

"What? Living here at the plantation, oh you have a right, you're Elena's son." He clapped him on the back then spoke,

"To be truthful, I'm a little jealous of you. Your mother was kind and so loving. What a life saver she was to me growing up, and especially after I lost my father. I was a lost soul just like you are now. Come on, let's get you settled in, and after we eat and you rest we'll talk some more."

Both walked into the dining area, and their food plates awaited them. The plantation was quiet and no one appeared as before. Only the clinking of silverware could be heard. Minutes later, Joel went to his room and Felicite motioned for the trunk and things in back of Joel's truck to be quietly taken to Joel's suite. Felicite continued his walk to the barn where he was to check on the last sugarcane deliveries headed out to New Orleans and sign off. He had promised he would do a follow-up call to Ms. Lolita Aime. He walked over to an empty stall and thought about Lolita wanting an Appaloosa colt. He flipped out his cell phone and made the necessary calls around and then to New York where a world-name breeder of the Appaloosa Friesian Blacks were bred with the American horses known for their colorful spotted coat. And Lolita was adamant in wanting a Friesian leopard-spot colt. She insisted all four of the socks of the colt be black. The breeder seemed to have several colts near the age of four fitting the required description. Felicite set up an appointment to come view their stock.

Joel wakened and surprisingly felt stronger. He looked out his bedroom window and noticed the winds had kicked up and the clouds were darkening. He reached for his cell phone and placed a call to the hospital to confirm his one o'clock appointment. Joel needed to sign on the dotted line of the contract to make his doctoring official at Mississippi's hospital. A few familiar exchanges were made as well as the confirmation of the time and place. He went outside to put his truck window up. He reached for the keys, turned the ignition on, and powered up the window, and not too soon. Big drops of rain splattered on him and the truck. He heard his name—well, nickname: "Hey, Dr. Northerner."

Joel turned in the sound's direction. It was his first cousin smiling from ear to ear. Joel felt at ease. That was part of Felicite's personality and it appeared he was joking. Joel hauled off running to the bungalow nestled to the far side of the barn. "Nice place. It's roomier than it looks on the outside."

"My father built this part," Felicite said, showing Joel the kitchen, bedroom, bath area, and the living room they were standing in. "I changed the front bedroom into a dining room and added another bath and three bedrooms. I'm all about rustic appearances. Most of the wood used came from right here on the plantation."

"Well, I'm impressed. You are multitalented."

Felicite placed his hands on his hips. "I am, and I like my privacy." Then he smiled and said, "Dr. Wright, I'm pleased you're making the plantation your home. Life in Mississippi is slower and maybe harder, but a person here is accepted by what he does and by his word and not anything else." He slapped Joel on the back. "Say, do you ever wear casual clothes?" Then he laughed.

"Call me Joel," he said, "and I have some store-bought clothes, remember Ms. Lolita Aime helped me with my purchase. I've also ordered several custom-made items."

Felicite gave him a once-over and said, "If you want to see where I shop, come with me sometime to Alabama."

Joel eyed his cousin and made a mental note to maybe check out Felicite's stores, but said, "I have to leave now. I have an appointment at the hospital. Looks like the rains are letting up." They walked outside.

Felicite said, "I have business up north and I'll be gone maybe a week, no more than two. Would you ride out with me later today where the cattle are grazing? I have a favor to ask."

From the truck, Joel said, "I should be back by four. I'll change and be ready."

Felicite nodded.

Joel backed the truck around in the drive and headed into town. He found the hospital without any trouble, being there was only one hospital to locate. He climbed the narrow steps and walked over to the receptionist area. "Hello, I'm Dr. Joel Taylor Wright. I'm here to see Mr. Chambers."

"Have a seat over there, anywhere, and I'll page him." The midsomething woman eyed him from head to toe and back again, then smiled. "Mr. Chambers, that city slicker you're expecting is here!"

Joel turned his head and sat down. He reached for a magazine to keep from squirming. He saw a short, balding man step up to the counter and laugh when he turned direction. His shirt sleeves were rolled up and his collar was unbuttoned. His slacks were slick from sitting and he wore cowboy boots. "Dr. Wright?" His hand thrust forward.

Joel gripped his hand and matched his strength.

"I'm Bob Chambers. Follow me."

Joel was served an iced tea and asked if the beginning of next month worked for him to come aboard at the hospital. He agreed and was handed a schedule, including the time of surgeries. Joel realized he would be precounseling with his patients, and asked, "Do I have a personal assistant nurse assigned to me or will it be the nurse of the day who works with me?"

Bob sipped his tea and set the glass down and scooted forward on his seat. "Dr. Wright, we are a little less formal here in the south than I'm sure you're used to, but our nursing staff on the cardiology floor are well equipped and could do what most doctors do if they were permitted. But don't say I said so. I'd have to pay them more." And he chuckled then stood.

Joel followed in pursuit and smiled. They walked together to the elevator, and Bob pushed the "up" button. Stepping inside, Bob said, "Welcome to our humble abode, your second home." On the fifth floor Bob, summoned the nursing staff together and introduced Dr. Joel Taylor Wright.

Joel nodded, smiled a lot, and eyed the female nurses, all three. He knew they were giving him the once-over more than once. The three nurses, a redhead, a brunette, and a silver-headed woman shook hands. He sided with the silver-headed one, who appeared to be married—well, at least she was wearing a wedding band. And he said, "I'm looking forward to being a part of this fine team and will appreciate your help any time with my patients, ladies. I'll see you next month." He straightened and walked with Bob into the surgical area. After the inspection of the operating room and state-of-the-art equipment, Joel reached out his hand to Bob and said, "Thank for your time today. I'm satisfied. Let's sign the paperwork, and I'll see you in January." After another thirty minutes, he pushed the elevator button and they rode down and walked to Bob's office. On his way out, Joel tipped his head to the blunt receptionist, but kept walking until he was behind the steering wheel of his truck. Joel was tempted to pull off his silk tie but didn't. He pulled around the back of the hospital's parking lot and watched the men doctors enter the emergency area, and saw how they were dressed.

At the plantation, Joel changed into jeans, a Cranbury shirt, and cowboy boots, and grabbed a fleece-lined coat and cowboy hat and hurried out to Felicite's office. "I'm here."

On horseback, they rode for forty-five minutes before Felicite said, "Look to your right. The whiteface cattle are our future stock, but we need a bull with a new bloodline. I'm thinking of adding Herefords to the mix for hardiness and thriftiness. It'll be money well spent." He lifted his hand and said, "The cattle in this field need to be transferred by next week to the new grazing field in the south pasture. Can you help out my right-hand man with the cattle transfer? But that's not all." As they rode along some time later, there was a field of more cattle.

Joel asked, "Why are these separated from the others?"

"The whitefaces in this pasture were raised for market. They need to be herded to the feeding lot and seen to that they have grain in front of them continually. Then by three months, they're off to auction. Our cattle usually bring in a good price."

"Sure, I'll help wherever I'm needed, but honestly, other than riding a horse that's the limit to my knowledge about a farm." He shifted in the saddle. "Where are you headed off to?"

Felicite turned his horse and motioned for Joel to do the same. "As I've indicated, I'm a very private man, but in all fairness, I'll be out of state attending to a request made by Lolita."

Joel's head turned in his cousin's direction, but the subject appeared to be a closed matter.

Felicite said, "Foreman's name is George," and chuckled, adding, "As was his father and his father before him, all the way back dating to our president George Washington." Eyebrows arched and his shoulders shrugged. "He's a good man and knows his way around cattle. Just you being there is support enough. And thank you for helping." Silence remained the rest of the ride. After rubbing down their horses, it was dinnertime and the men scurried to their living quarters to tidy up.

Joel in business attire made his way to the dining area. Felicite was changed and said, "George, this is my cousin, Dr. Joel Taylor Wright. He will be riding with you to oversee the cattle move."

Joel eyed the brown-eyed man with medium-dark olive skin, and extended his smooth hand to George. "Call me Joel, please, and so nice to meet you."

George smiled and grabbed Joel's hand. "We'll head out at five in the morning."

Joel glanced over at Felicite and back toward George and said, "I'll be ready."

The men set down and ate. After the meal, Joel and Felicite went into the drawing room for a nightcap and talk. Joel said, "I'm planning on a lengthy project myself, but first of all, are the small cabins we passed today occupied?"

"No." He scrubbed his face. "Why?"

"Just a thought, but first I'm having added plumbing to the house. The plantation's bathrooms need toilets and bathtubs. Things need to be brought up to code and into our generation."

"That's a huge oversee."

"I'm having an architect fly in to go over my plans, hoping to join the old and the new ideas together. I can see why mother bought this place and her love for it."

"Well, Joel, don't bite off more than you can chew." He stood and said, "I'm turning in. I have an early flight tomorrow. See you in a week or two." He clapped Joel on the shoulder and added, "You'll need your beauty sleep, for tomorrow will be a hard day. Oh, I asked Elsa to pack you a breakfast and lunch with a thermos of black coffee. You'll need it before the day is over."

The men went their separate ways, and Joel laid out his work clothing for the next day. He hung his suit up and slid his shoes into the narrow closet, thinking, *Another item to improve upon— closet space.* He lit a fire in the fireplace and dressed down to his briefs and slid into his king-sized bed. His six-two frame stretched out, and sleep was settling in. Then Lolita's face appeared before him. He woke in a sweat and sat straight up, now 2:30 a.m. Work would come all too soon. He saw Felicite's truck head down the lane to destinations unknown and for Lolita. Could both men have feelings for the same woman? What's more, could the woman have feelings for both men? He lay on the bed and hit his pillow, willing sleep to come.

His watch ring-a-dinged and Joel scurried from bed. He met Elsa at the door with a sack in hand and a thermos filled with black coffee. George was waiting with the cattle herdsmen on horseback. He held out the reins to Joel. After the pasture came into sight, the ropes and yelps began. It was giddyup and roundup time for sure. Halfway into the day, Joel was feeling the pain and strain from being in the saddle and whirling his right arm up in the air. Almost two thousand cattle had been transferred to the grazing pasture. Calves were bawling, cows were mooing, and he sympathized with them. George and the hands stretched after the gate was locked and the water tanks were filled and the grain buckets set in place. Joel saw the men eating jerky and he opened his sack to find and apple and an orange. Some meal for the day. George gave a disturbing, eerie whistle, and the men mounted their horses and so did he. The ride was long and the herding was slow. The whiteface cattle seemed restless, as if they sensed the road they were to travel would be short. Several times, the men had to run interference with the young bulls. Their long horns of three to five feet were impressive and scary. But George and the men roped and tag-teamed the herd, until late that night the cattle were in the feeding lot. Joel saw row after row of grainy bins and filled water troughs. The cattle were almost neck to neck. Very little movement could they make. George said, "It will take a good three months to fatten up this stock for auction."

Joel noticed the manmade roofs to shelter the cattle and the straw to place under their hoofs should a rain or need come. Joel surmised there were a thousand head. The sun had set and the horses still needed to be rubbed down, fed, and watered. He didn't know if he could put one foot in front of the other. Joel had a different respect for his cousin, one of adoration; no wonder Felicite didn't need a gym. He hit his cowboy hat on his leg and the dust flew. George said, "Joel, the stable hands will care for our horses tonight. Let's clean up and go eat."

Joel liked what he heard. He smiled and nodded. He blinked, and the men were out of sight. Joel wanted a long, hot shower, but in eight minutes flat he was washed, dressed, and glazing the steps to the dinner table. The men laughed and jostled with each other and included him. He bantered back and forth and felt happier than he had ever remembered. Elsa's fried chicken, mashed potatoes, brown gravy, and long green string beans with homemade biscuits were awesome. Joel even took a second helping and didn't consider any guilt. He passed on the drawing room and went straight upstairs to his bedroom. Once again hung up his business attire and headed for the shower. The heated water rolled down his back and across his shoulders. He let the spray hit his face and rested his hands against the shower walls. Joel toweled and shaved and once again laid out his clothes for the next day. The architect would be arriving after 10:00 a.m.

7

FELICITE PARKED HIS truck in the designated parking area and walked into the airport. His flight number was posted and appeared to be on time. He carried his duffel bag on the plane, placed it in the overhead area, and sat down and fidgeted in his seat until the plane landed. Inside the New York airport he was greeted by the horse breeder, Johnson, and he offered to drive them to the farm. Felicite hopped in, and several hours later they arrived. Some horses were grazing, some in a training area, and some were stationary in their massive stable that was air-conditioned and heated as needed. Felicite saw newborn fillies with their moms, and in a closed area, in the triple-wide barn, stood two Appaloosa colts, separated by a temporary fence. To their side, hay stood, and a chestnut mare with a cream-colored mane and tail and four matching socks. She was beautiful and very pregnant. She drew him in to reach and touch. Her coat was smooth and soft. The man said, "She's for sale. The history behind retired Clare May is that she jumped the fence and had a rendezvous with Sir Grislier the third. An established, sought-after breeding stallion, Clara May was not expected to be impregnated and certainly not carry her foal to full term, yet here she is, and without a worthy pedigree. The foal will not be worth much either, so do you want to make an offer, package deal, mare and foal-to-be?"

Felicite tipped his Stetson hat and placed a foot on the rail, then grunted, "I don't rightly know." Shifting feet, pointed out to the colts. "Are these the three-year-old colts we spoke about over the phone?"

"They are. Here's their pedigrees. Sir Chancellor sired Chyboon, and Sir Grislier sired Channel. Both stallions are well sought after, worldwide they have won national and world entries."

Felicite made a mental note that Chyboon had no affiliation to Clara May's fold.

And the fact that Chyboon had the most black marks across his shoulders and rear and that he had the four black socks, and the other colt had some graying through the mane and tail. He said, "Mind taking me to a hotel and I'll think on these matters and get back to you tomorrow? I would like to spend time watching their movements and how they deal with a lead."

"Sure. There are motels up the way, and in the next town over there a five-star hotel."

"Motel will be fine!"

That night, Felicite did an online search with the information he had from the horse breeder. The asking price for the three-four-year-old colts were $6,500.00 each. He also thought over rather buying Clara May. His mind asked why, and his heart won over for the mare. She had soul and was comforting to him. He questioned: what if the mare died giving birth and he lost both horse and foal? But then what if he didn't? Wish he could be certain if the foal was a filly? Only a 40 percent chance, since the record is high in siring colts. Asking price $1,200.00 dollars for mare and unborn. Mother-to-be was twelve years old and had no known births before.

After his restless night's sleep, Felicite called a cab and went to the Johnson breeder's farm. He watched and interacted with the colts, and saw that Chyboon was the gentler one of the two and seemed more adaptable to learn his type of teaching, while Channel was more on the headstrong side and not so shy. So, based on a hunch and his love for animals, Felicite thought Chyboon would be the better foal for Lolita and would adapt quickly. He offered $5,500.00 for the colt and a thousand for the pregnant mare. More negotiations were made and finally an agreement came: $6,000.00 for the colt and a $1,050.00 for Clara May. They shook hands and then the breeder signed the legal papers and offered to deliver both purchases for an additional delivery fee of $1,500.00 and a five-day delivery. "Normally the trip would be made in three days, but with the mare in her condition, slow would be best."

Felicite said, "Done deal. See you in a week." He pulled out his wallet and paid in cash. Shook hands again and placed his papers in his jacket's front pocket and asked the man to call a cab.

Felicite had circled back to the motel to pick up his tote bag and had the cab driver take him to the busy New York airport. Inside the airport, he was only too happy to be carrying a tote bag. A half hour later, he sat aboard his flight, and in two hours and forty-four minutes the plane landed in New Orleans. He called Lynen before landing and asked, "Have a room for me tonight," drawing out her name, "Ms. Aime."

"Felicite, I was only expecting a follow-up phone call about the delivered sugarcane. Where are you?"

"At the New Orleans airport."

"Whatever are you doing there? Need Lolita to come pick you up?"

"No. I'll take a cab."

"You get yourself here now, dinner will be waiting!"

Chuckling, he said, "I'm on my way, and thanks, ma'am." Although it wasn't a long drive, it was time consuming. People loved to party and the streets were full. When he arrived at the B & B, he paid the cab driver, lifted his tote, and headed toward the front door. Felicite tapped on the door and a robed Lynen answered. She was coughing and holding her head. He entered and asked, "Have you seen the doctor?"

Motioning him inside, she said, "No, been too busy." She swayed. Felicite reached out and took matters into his own hands. He flipped out his cell phone and called an ambulance. Lolita came rushing into the foyer and helped sit her mother down. "Lolita, why haven't you seen that your mother went to the doctor?" The sirens were close. The eerie, piercing sounds always sent chills up his back.

"I'm sorry, Felicite. I didn't realize she was that bad. I thought she only had a little cold."

The medics stepped in the B & B's foyer and didn't wait for anyone to speak. They lowered the stretcher, up went Ms. Aime. They started an IV and placed an oxygen mask over her nose, then gave her a shot to calm her down. She passed out. The medics rushed her out of the B & B, and Felicite belted, "Lolita, I'll go with your mother. You keep everything here on schedule. I'll call you when they get her settled." He hopped into the ambulance and the red light flashed and the sirens sounded and they moved in and out of traffic.

Felicite stayed at the check-in desk before entering the ER to answer what questions he could about his dear friend, Lynen, while they wheeled her on into a side room. She looked so frail instead of overwhelmingly intimidating. He was given permission to visit Lynen, and he stayed by her side for hours. Finally the doctor came in with updated reports. Pneumonia. Her lungs were so full they were having a hard time taking in air and releasing it. The oxygen level was raised to a six. A clear oxygen tent was placed over her, and Lynen was moved to an isolated room. Everyone entering wore a mask, cloth gown, plastic gloves, and blue shielded things over their shoes. He had fifteen texts from Lolita. He needed to update her and knew his trip home to the plantation would be delayed. He went to the area where phone calls could be made.

"Hello, Joel? Yes, I know what time it is. Listen, I'm in New Orleans and Ms. Lynen Aime is in the hospital with pneumonia.

Yes, it's serious, and if you're any kind of a praying man now would be the time to pray."

"Do you need my help or connections?" Joel asked.

"Thank you, Joel, but no. At least not yet. I do need you to be at the plantation. Saturday midmorning I have a delivery coming, a colt and a bred mare, and have the vet there on standby. Clara May's pregnancy is risky, and the mare needs to have an ultrasound. It's her first delivery, and the ole gal may not make it through this. Have our stable hand to have the yard and a stall ready for the young colt. He's a bit shy, but watch out, he nibbles. Be extra kind to Clara May. She's a beauty and will need a quiet stall with lots of straw. If there's any difficulty, call me. I'm counting on you, coz." The connection was cut.

Felicite went down to the cafeteria and grabbed an apple and a black coffee then placed a call to Lolita. "Hello. Calm down. Is everything at the B & B all right?"

"Yes."

"All right then. I think it wise to call in an industrial cleaning staff to cleanse the B & B. Your mother has pneumonia. All her sheets, bedding, towels, clothes, you know the drill—and you wear a mask until walls, floors, everything has been sanitized. Are you up on your shots?"

"I am, Felicite. And thank you for looking after the both of us, but I'm a big girl."

"Hey, I'm not the shining knight here. You would do the same for me. That's what friends are for." He heard his name announced and he ended their call. Chugging down the coffee, he stood and walked toward the elevator. Inside, he felt the loneliness and a force bigger than himself pulled him into prayer. "Haven't talked with you much since dad died, but this isn't for me, it's for Lynen Aime. Strengthen her and give comfort." The door opened. He stepped out and headed down the hall where he was requested to check in.

The suited-up doctor in disposable whites said, "I need to check you out as a precaution."

"What? I'm healthy as an old bull."

The stern doctor said, "Strip. The nurse will be in here shortly to take your vital signs and blood." The doctor disappeared.

He hated hospital gowns and their openness. He fumbled with the stupid ties and their match-ups. A nurse dressed more like an alien walked into his room. "Lie down, sir." She covered him from the waist down with a sheet and asked, "Have you kept up with your routine shots?"

He said, "I had my flu and pneumonia shots in October. I'm good."

She stuck a needle in his forearm and filled five tubes with blood. "That ought to do." She smiled and said, "Wait here. Don't get dressed until you've been cleared." She whisked from the room.

He could do nothing but wait, so he reached for his Stetson hat and placed it over his eyes, hoping to catch a catnap. Someone touched his arm. "Felicite Tomas?"

He jerked upward, cowboy hat hitting the floor, and gown gaping. He clutched the front and glanced in the direction of the voice. He found a young, good-looking nurse eyeing him, and deeply. She was so close he could smell her light floral fragrance. He didn't dare speak; their lips would touch. He stared, sitting spine-straight. She lifted her frame from listening to his heart rate and said, "You can get dressed now. You're healthy." She batted her lashes and asked, "Need any help?"

He did a quick intake of air and said with a slow smile, "Maybe another time, ma'am."

She swayed from the room, and Felicite let out a held breath, then said, "And I thought I look like crap, unshaven, unshowered, and in the same clothes worn at the horse farm. Go figure out, women." He dressed and hurried to Lynen's room. Still in an oxygen tent, asleep. He checked in at the nurses' station and asked how she was doing.

"What we can tell you is that she is in a weakened condition, but for her age she's a fighter. Unless she has a sedative, she is scrappy. The next four or five days will tell the story."

He thanked the nurses and walked down to her room, put on the disposable clothing provided and slipped into her room. Wearing a mask, he placed his hand through a small opening and squeezed her small, pale, callused hand. "Hey, Lynen, you're looking better today, a bit more color. How's the doctor treating you?"

Of course he knew she wouldn't and couldn't answer, but it felt like the right thing to do. So he teased, "I saw your silver-haired doctor in charge hanging around this morning and again when I came in this afternoon. He's way too invested in you as a patient. He's charmed by you. Watch it, Ms. Aime, or you won't always be single." He chuckled and patted her hand. He stayed several hours then decided on a break, knowing he needed to leave, shower, shave, and change his funky clothes. However, the silver-haired doctor rounded the corner, in his street clothing, and Felicite watched as the fine doctor stopped outside Lynen's door.

At the B & B, Lolita hugged Felicite and hung on. He said, "Your mother is stronger today. And in a few days it will make a big difference. After I clean up we'll talk some more. I have some great news for you. Which room am I in?"

"Can't you tell me now?" she snapped.

"No. Later."

"Room six. I'll have a tray sent to your room."

"Lolita, if I'm not down here by 4:00 p.m., come wake me."

Felicite rubbed his eyes; they were sensitive to the sun shining through the window. His cell phone rang. "Joel, what's up? What's all that pounding?"

"The mare and the Appaloosa colt have arrived, as well as the veterinarian. He has stuck like glue to the mare. He gave that tired-out old mare an ultrasound and the colt appears to be a filly. He isn't sure she can deliver safely and certainly not without help. What were you thinking buying an aged mare and what about the new colt? He's gorgeous, though."

"Joel, the colt is for Lolita. The mare, well, she has loving eyes." He laughed. "What is all that noise?"

Joel said, "I flew in an architect to the plantation and am having rooms reconstructed and redesigned, as well as another wing built on to the plantation, along with all modernizing of the indoor plumbing. The seven cabins are next for an overhaul, and we can use the cabins for future guests. Some will showcase two bedrooms and the others will showcase only one, but all the cabins will have an eat-in area and a bathroom, which will be fully equipped when done, more on the rustic style. I have an idea I want to run by you when you return. Say, when is that day?"

"Yes, we need to talk! I have a few ideas myself about the project."

Joel interrupted, "Got to go Felicite, the vet's calling me. I think it's Clare May."

Felicite wanted to stay angry at Lolita for letting him sleep in, but he was to glad to feel refreshed and rested. His clothes were cleaned and lay on a chair. He washed his face and left his scruffy beard. Then he called the hospital.

The attending nurse said, "Lynen breathing on a lower level of oxygen and her coloring appears almost normal. Your friend is in good hands."

In the dining room, he caught Lolita's eye. She sat down at the table and waited until he finished with the meal.

"All right, tell me the news." Lolita folded her hands in her lap.

Felicite reached for his cell phone and opened his photos. Lolita squealed when she saw her Leopard Appaloosa with his four black socks. "Oh, Felicite, great job on the colt selection, he's everything and more. He looks so strong and willful. Is he named?"

"Yes, his name is Chyboon. His sire is brilliant, strong, blue–black, and has won national and world-wide trophies. He's a little shy for a stallion." He lifted from the table with her hand in his. He kissed it and said, "I must be off to the hospital," and kissed her cheek. The cab was called. Felicite was faced with his friend lying in the same room, same IVs, and same oxygen tent, but she was moving her mouth to the silver-haired doctor. Felicite suited up and said, "Hello, doctor"—turning to the woman—"Lynen."

The doctor stood, patted her hand, and left the room. Lynen's eyes rolled in Felicite's direction, and she half smiled. "I'm glad to see you in better spirits." He saw her oxygen had been lowered to a level 2; definitely an improvement. Felicite sat down and reached for her hand. "The welcoming news is that if you keep showing healthy progress, you're going home."

"I'd like nothing more. Sorry to have scared you."

He shook his head and patted her hand, "You're a stubborn woman, Ms. Aime." Then Felicite smiled.

"I'm hungry. They're starving me to death."

A full laugher came from Felicite. He said, "Let me see what I can do for you." He rose and left the room. Soon nurses and the lurking silver-haired doctor saw that the tent was removed, and that she was bathed, and a light meal was served. One soft egg, Jell-O, and one slice of wheat bread. No salt, pepper, or butter—all bland. But Lynen ate and sobbed up her plate. "More."

Felicite chuckled and relaxed a little; his friend would recover. While the x-ray and more blood work was done, he went to the cafeteria. He took from the serving bar a salad, two hard-boiled eggs, a banana, orange juice, and a large hot black coffee. Felicite sat down in a quiet corner ate and, while sipping his coffee, called Joel. Third ring: "How's Clara May?"

"You should ask. She is in labor and the vet is getting ready. The foreman and hands are all on standby. I've stopped the work on the plantation house and the cottages. You know, no noise for our girl. She's growing on me."

Felicite let out an audible sigh. "Are you whispering sweet nothings in her ear?"

"Are you watching me?" Changing the subject, Joel asked, "How is Ms. Lynen Aime?"

"Slowly improving, and perhaps under doctor's care can go home soon." He was tempted to say something on his thoughts about her doctor, but didn't; that could wait. "I'm hoping to be back the day after tomorrow. Did you get all the cattle transferred?"

"We did. I'm still in serious physical pain. I'll use my brain any day over your brawn."

Both laughed. "The mare is lying down again. Got to go." Joel pushed the cell's end button.

Felicite went back to the nurses' station for a further update on Lynen Aime. He saw that the silver-haired doctor was standing by and asked, "In your professional opinion, how is Lynen Aime?"

"Mr. Tomas, she is getting stronger, and the antibiotic seems to be working. Matter of fact, she is doing quite well. If she keeps on improving I'll release her in the morning. She is in a different room now. The nurse will fill you in. I'm being paged."

Felicite was given her room number and was happy to see Lynen sitting up and in good color. "Look at you!"

She smiled and said, "I'm going home tomorrow. Felicite, thank you for your care."

"Ah, nothing." He made small chitchat, then went on about the colt he found for Lolita and showed her pictures from his cell phone. Lynen's smile deepened, reaching her eyes, and she touched the screen. "He's magnificent."

8

LOLITA HIRED ANOTHER housekeeper and several maids to work at the B & B. She also brought on staff a nurse to care for her mother. She saw that the boarders were settled and enjoying the never-sleeping New Orleans. Felicite stayed another night. He met with Lynen the next morning in the parlor and closed the door. "I understand you and Joel didn't part on good terms. Is that so?"

"He's arrogant and self-centered, just like his father," she huffed out.

"Lynen, I beg to differ with you. Joel has just lost both his parents, found out his background and heritage is different than he was raised to believe, and he's inherited multiple properties, changed living places and employment. The only one thing stable in the man's life is his work." He began pacing. "Joel's move to the plantation has done wonders. He's bringing in needed plumbing and having restoration done where needed. My cousin has covered for me on roundup with the cattle and has carried out all requests made of him."

"Well."

Felicite reached for her hands and sat down looking her in the hurtful eyes. "Do you remember anything about the loss of my father? Joel's mother left her family and her society events to come to my aid. She was caring and loving and helped me out in a dark time. Joel didn't get that from anyone, and he is questioning his acceptance anywhere. So why wouldn't he be blatant? I've reconsidered my thoughts about our Northerner and I am finding him to be reliable, mannerly, and quite entertaining." He lifted from the chair, kissed her on the cheek, and said, "You need your bed rest and that was your doctor's orders. I'm heading back to the plantation. I've got a mare in labor and she's in difficulty."

"How you getting home?" Lynen whispered.

Just then a tap came on the doorway. It was Lolita with the silver-haired doctor. He nodded to Felicite and said, "Ms. Aime, how are you feeling today?"

"Well, you're the doctor," she giggled.

"Ms. Aime." Taking a big gulp of air, he said, "I'm not here as your doctor today. I'm…I'm…" He blew out a breath. "I wish to ask you out on a date when you're doing better. Perhaps next week, when the playhouse is presenting *A Time to Dance*. I would like for you to attend with me." He waited with hands placed behind his back.

Lolita glanced over to Felicite, and they both began smiling. Lynen said, "Dr. Bennett, you may call me by my first name, Lynen. And yes, I would like to accept your invitation to the play."

Audible sighs were heard in the room.

"Lynen, thank you, and you may call me Joppa, or Joe for short."

Lynen yawned, and the doctor said, "I'm afraid I've stay too long and tired you." He smiled and touched her cheek. "I'll call you tomorrow."

He rang for the nurse and walked out the door, letting himself out.

The nurse came in and helped Lynen to her feet. But Lynen stopped outside the door, and looked at Lolita. "Dear, the B & B is well covered, and thanks to you we have a nurse on staff that will look after me, so you take Felicite home." She raised her frail hand and added, "No ands, ifs, or buts. After all, I have a doctor on call." A giggle slipped out.

"All right, mother, but I'll return later tonight."

"No. Don't be stubborn. Felicite has a mare in labor and that poor Northerner doctor is at his wit's end helping the veterinarian out, and what does he know, he's a cardiologist, and this is his first animal delivery." Her mother swayed and Felicite lifted her in his arms and carried her to her bedroom. Lolita covered her with a light blanket and the nurse shooed them from the room. "I've got this."

Both Felicite and Lolita listened by the door. The nurse asked, "Lynen, would like a drink of cool water?" before closing the bedroom door and eyeing Lolita and Felicite.

Lolita warmed the engine of the two-door jeep and motioned for Felicite to hop in. He was all smiles and resorted to his quiet self. An hour down the highway, Lolita said, "So, can I see my colt when I get there? Is he halter-trained? When will you begin training him, right away?"

"Whoa…I know you're excited and should be. The stallion is strong, smart, and brilliantly marked, and he is a bit shy, but teachable. I would possibly like to use him to breed later on. What are your thoughts?" He shifted in the seat.

"Oh, Felicite, of course you can use him as a sire. After all, you paid for him, and all I'm paying for is his boarding." She glanced his way. "What's this about a mare in labor?"

He lifted his Stetson and resettled it on his thick, wavy auburn hair. "While up north searching for the colt for you, I saw her, Clara May. Her eyes are warm, the color of molasses. She's sweet, gentle, and I am in love. She older and a first-time mother-to-be, and I'm afraid a little bit, skittish. Clara May is smooth and soft to the touch. The vet is with her now, hope I make it there before she delivers. Maybe I can help."

"You could deliver the foal yourself, with all the cattle you've assisted with over the years."

"Thanks for the vote of confidence. I feel Joel is a big help in this matter. His bedside manners can be right on."

"You're joking?"

"As I was telling your mother"—Felicite stretched—"Joel right now is a lost soul, with losing both parents, finding out his heritage is different than the way he was brought up. And suddenly he's been faced with so many decisions, what to do with the properties, and questioning how to fit in without real family, except me." He lifted his hat. "Joel changed location and employment. There's more to him than when he first appeared. And I'm finding out that we are more alike than we ever thought."

She stared at him, and Felicite grabbed the wheel. "Maybe you should let me drive."

To his surprise, Lolita pulled over and got out, fanning herself. Felicite reached the Mississippi line when Lolita asked, "What are your plans in using Chyboon to sire? Oh, I know he's too young now, but when he's older."

"I need to speak with Joel first, then we'll talk."

"Felicite, but why? Joel's so indecisive."

He locked brown eyes to brown eyes and said, "Joel's had to make a lot of decisions in the last two months. Maybe he's being wise staying away from you. You're not serious in your thinking about Joel, are you?" He chuckled then continued, "You're upset he didn't chase after you. I warned you, chérie, we love them and leave them."

She punched his arm.

Felicite pretended the hit hurt, then laughed as he drove up the dirt driveway and parked her jeep in front of the stable. "Lolita, don't cause trouble and keep quiet in the stables. Remember the mare." He smiled and hugged her. "Thanks for the lift."

"Hey, Felicite, I hope that is you." Joel was rubbing the neck of the mare and was whispering in her ear.

"Where's the vet?"

Clara May whinnied, and Joel said, "I need your help in turning the foal so both have a chance to live. Clara May is worn out."

Felicite knelt and twisted on the mare's stomach as Joel turned his hands inside the mare. Lolita began rubbing the mare and saying soothing things of encouragement to her. Joel, in almost a whisper, said, "The vet received a call from the next farm over. Their black Angus bull was cut when trying to jump the bob wire fence. And at that time Clare May was the same as when you and I last spoke. I camped out here with her last night, and right before dawn she let out a terrible piercing cry. My specialty is the heart, but I've also delivered a baby or two. Clara May's foal is still lodged sideways." Just then Clara May tried to get up. Felicite threw his body across her and Joel pulled at the foal. Between both men, the foal turned and was born, face first. Clara May rose to her feet and nestled her foal, a filly. Lolita brought a bucket of cold water for the men to wash up, but Felicite pulled Joel out of the stable and poured the water over his head. "You looked like you're going to pass out."

Joel laughed—really laughed—and grabbed Felicite's shirttail and flung him to the ground. Both wrestled rolled and romped around, until neither one could move, just laugh.

Lolita, with hands on her curvy hips, said, "Men!" and she stomped off to the other side of the stable where her colt, Chyboon, stood. She reached up to the halter and then carefully let him sniff, before patting his neck. With gentle movements she said, "You're so beautiful and so magnificently marked." She let out an audible, "Ah," then said, "My very own Appaloosa Friesian Leopard colt." She placed her other arm around his neck for a hug. Chyboon slightly kicked at the ground, but stood still, as if he enjoyed her gushy words and affection.

Meanwhile, Joel and Felicite stood at the stall and watched both mother and foal bond. The dust from the driveway kicked up and they turned to see the vet park. He was amazed to hear how Joel used his doctor skills to aid in delivering the foal. He said, "We might make you into a Southerner yet." He glanced over at Joel, adding, "I wasn't born here either, but I love the laid-backness and the hospitality of the south. I'm originally from New York. Couldn't tell, could ya?"

Joel shook his head. "How long have you been in Mississippi?"

"Twenty or so years."

The hammering began and Felicite whipped around. "So what's being done on the plantation house?"

"Adding another wing, ten bedrooms with attached modern bathrooms. The main kitchen is being brought to a chief's desire, with both hot and cold water." Joel placed his hands on his narrow hips and added, "Elsa has stood firm with the crew and taken lead in overseeing all the new kitchen gadgets, utensils, pots, pans, and kettles that will be brought in." He shrugged his shoulders. "Felicite, will you ride with me later and view the cottages?"

"Sure. I have something I want to run by you too."

Joel nodded. "Four thirty, then, right before dinner?"

The vet handed Felicite a prescription with instructions to give the mare, and said, "Clara May needs molasses in her feed and she needs to eat three times a day to build up her health and strength. Hay won't hurt either in her stall for now instead of straw."

"Will the prescription hurt the foal as she drinks from his mother's milk?" Felicite inquired.

"No, all natural medicine. These vitamins are to be dropped into her water. Use as instructed for two weeks then stop."

The three men glanced back at the pair, foal and mother. And an overwhelming peace hummed in the air, silence, until Lolita said, "Looks like you're good at something, Dr. Northerner."

His blue eyes sparkled with a darkness that held her mysterious brown eyes. The electricity traveled between them and he saw her grab the rail. Then she blinked and stared back at his eyes and they suddenly revealed nothing. She excused herself and forced herself to slow down her steps. Inside the house, she realized she was breathing hard. And looking in the mirror, saw she was flushed. Lolita checked with Elsa to see if a room was available and if she could turn on the water.

Elsa tucked her brown hands in her apron pocket and belted, "Girl, you should check with the owner. However"—lowing her husky voice—"Let's get you settled in the newest wing." She fluffed her apron and continued talking, "That Dr. Wright has amazing talents. He's a lot like his mother, who saw a vision for the plantation, but, bless her soul, she never got to act upon it." Elsa opened the wide, massive mission's door and said, "Here's your suite for the night. Excuse the light paint smell. The windows are up, still airing. See you at dinner." Elsa backed from the room.

Lolita fingered the artwork hung by Joel's mother and looked at the soft blue–painted walls and crisp white bedding. "It's all so appealing. Modern, yet quaint." She waltzed into the bathroom and there stood a claw-foot tub, a separate shower, and an old vintage dresser that had been made into a washing area with a large copper sink. It had plenty of storage. She spotted a basket full of toiletries, salts, fragrant oils, and spicy and floral bubble bath. Personal items, razors, scented little soaps, toothbrush, toothpaste, and, men's and women's deodorant was added and sitting on a saucer. She turned on the hot water just a little to test it; it was hot to the touch. She giggled and lowered the plug then turned on the cold water tap and let them both run at once. She added spice and bubbles to the water and slipped off her clothes. Down into the alluring waters she unfolded. Lolita unwrapped one of the tiny soaps and it felt creamy to her skin. After rinsing she let some water out of tub then turned on the hot water and laid back her head to relax. Sleep invaded.

Felicite and Joel met and rode horses to the cabin grounds. Both dismounted and went inside a finished cabin. Felicite removed his Stetson and view the changes to the place. He said, "What do you have in mind for the rest of the cabins?"

Smiling, Joel, with hand out, said, "Since I've been here at the plantation I've been more relaxed, and I was thinking that city folks might enjoy spending a special week or weekend here. Perhaps we could carve out a blazing horse trail, a campout area for meals, or maybe entertain an old-fashioned hoedown. The money charged for the stay would pay for the help needed, added horses, maybe even see our land differently? What are your thoughts?"

Felicite stared at Joel, then said, "I really believe you're on to something, and that mentioning horses is funny in a way, for I'm hoping to develop a horse line of Appaloosas, and wanted to offer riding lessons. That was one of the reasons I bought the mare. Wait, not to necessarily ride the mare, but use her foal to breed with Lolita's colt when it's time."

Joel smiled. "Well, we have a good number of horses now, and if the lines are improved that's a plus. Felicite, would you be game for us to start up a resort/retreat? And perhaps we would be giving back to the community somewhat. You know, people going into town and shopping for that special souvenir."

"When will all the cabins be completed?" Felicite held his hands up.

"Hopefully in two more months, if the carpentry gets finished, then a decorator will need to be hired."

They shook hands and clapped each other on the back. "What a businessman you are, my cousin."

"Not so bad yourself, Felicite." They mounted their horses and Joel said, "So by midspring, we should be able to schedule our first outing. We'll need an advertising campaign to spread the word of our retreat/resort. Boy, do I hope the crops and cattle don't interfere with our timing."

"We can always hire more help?" Felicite said.

At the stable, Felicite and Joel stood outside the stall admiring the newborn colt. Then Felicite turned toward Joel. "Say, Lolita could help with decorative design. She studied art abroad and could bring a good eye to the cabin's perspective."

Joel whipped around and without hesitation said, "No."

Felicite chuckled. "Coz, there's plenty of time. Come on, let's get cleaned up and head in to eat."

Joel headed to his suite, but Elsa stopped him and said, "There's water running in the new wing."

A few minutes later, Joel gave a light tap on a suite's door, but there wasn't any answer. He walked into the suite, for the door wasn't locked, and looked around the room. It was quiet and dark, the drapes pulled closed. He turned on the lower light and edged quietly into the bathroom where the tub was overflowing and threatening to be a huge problem if left to continue. He reached for the water spigots and turned them off. And twisted his body and glanced across the tub.

She yelled, "What do you think you're doing in here?" She started to stand.

His blue eyes were glued. Lolita pointed to the hanging towel and said, "Be a gentleman and hand me the towel."

He obeyed, but didn't move. She stood with a large towel wrapped around her frame and said, "Dr. Northerner." Then she saw the water on the floor and began crying, "Oh no, I must have fallen asleep. I'm sorry."

Joel knew the new floor repair would be costly, but her sincerity drew him nearer to her. He reached his large hand to her face and tilted it up and bent and kissed her lips. Then, just as quickly he pulled back and cleared his throat. "Ms. Aime, dinner is being served. Don't worry about the bathroom." He placed several towels down for her to step onto, but the water was still too deep. He swept her up in his arms and carried her to the bed. Eyeing her bare shoulders and glanced at her red-painted toenails, he said, "The bathroom will be good as new by the time you're ready to retire." He left the suite and let the door slam. Three long steps in the corridor, he inhaled and slowly released the air. Joel couldn't quit trembling. She had a strange effect on him, and her creamy skin called out to every cell in him to touch. No other woman, and there had been many, had ever soothed and spiked his temper from zero to ten in less than a minute. He lifted his cell phone and called the construction company. "I don't care that you're closed for the night. The plantation has a flood problem in one of the new suites and I expect it to be fixed within the hour." He inhaled again and paced his walk.

After dinner, Felicite, Lolita, and Joel went into the drawing room. Felicite kept the conversation flowing. He glanced at Lolita and then over at Joel, whose faced was masked from any expression. He knew that look; he'd been there before himself with women. Although Lolita seemed irritated, maybe frustrated, she smiled from time to time. He watched Joel set his drink down when Elsa entered the room and said, "Dr. Wright, there's someone waiting for you in the foyer." She fluffed her apron. Joel excused himself from the drawing room, thinking it was the construction person. He almost stumbled when he heard, "There you are. I've missed you." Her words were cooing, and when he opened his mouth to speak, he realized Felicite was standing behind him.

"Cousin, who's this lovely woman? You're not planning on keeping her all to yourself, are you?" His brown eyes twinkled. Felicite stepped forward and kissed the petite woman's hand and bowed. "Madame, I'm at your service."

Joel saw Lolita swift by in her green plaid taffeta dress and her brown eyes were fiery and squinted. Her dress rustled and the hair at the back of his neck rose. He said, "Let me have the honor of introducing you to each other. Ms. Jewels Romany, meet my cousin Mr. Felicite Tomas." Nodding, Joel continued, "Jewels is an acquaintance of mine from Columbus, Ohio. She's an airline steward for National High Air."

She whined, "Joel, be a dear and pay the cab driver and bring in my luggage."

He flinched, but went out to the cab.

Felicite offered his arm and asked, "Have you eaten dinner, Ms. Romany?"

She eyed him and touched his arm, batting her eyelashes, and flashing her green eyes. "Call me Jewels."

He patted her hand on his arm. "We were about to have dessert." He turned slightly, raised a hand, and rang for Elsa.

Within moments, she entered the room.

"We have a house guest for the night. Will you see that Ms. Romany has a suite? And dinner would be nice. We'll take our dessert and her dinner in the dining hall. Thank you, Elsa."

She puffed her brown lips and fluffed her apron, huffing while making her way down the hall. Jewels followed her. In the dining hall, Lolita was seated and waited for the threesome to appear. When Joel came back inside the house with his arms full of luggage he found just Felicite still in the foyer. Joel thundered, "I didn't know Jewels was coming. I haven't been in touch with her for months."

Felicite said, "She's staying in the east wing, one floor under yours. But what I want to know is, is there anything serious between the two of you?" He paced back and forth.

"No, Felicite. That ship sailed a long time ago. We were never a permanent item, if that's what you're asking, just a casual fling, honest. I can't imagine her showing up here like this, unannounced."

"Why, Joel, you're a bachelor who is wealthy and has been much publicized with the death of your parents and all." He studied Joel then spoke. "Would your feathers get ruffled if I approached the lady? Wow, she's a piece of art, and her bewitching green eyes—green eyes have always been a weakness of mine." Felicite placed a hand over his heart.

Joel began chuckling. "Be my guest. I'm really not interested in that woman, Jewels. My wants and desires have moved on."

9

A DINNER BELL was rung and both men knew to go into the dining hall. Felicite watched the ladies, Lolita and Jewels, interact. Lolita was a perfect host, but her brown eyes were throwing darts. He glanced at Joel and saw him running a finger around his shirt collar; other than that, he would not have known of Joel's discomfort. Felicite observed Joel being surprisingly polite and even charming. Suddenly Joel's neck muscles flexed when Jewels asked him if they could talk privately. Joel stood and bowed, before thinking of his Northern ways. He extended his arm and she looped hers around his. They, in quietness, walked into the drawling room. The servant poured Joel a short drink and offered the woman a hot tea. She said, "I'd like a glass of white wine, please."

The servant glanced in Joel's direction and he nodded. The servant left the room and returned carrying a glass filled with white substance on a tray.

"Thank you, sir."

He nodded, bowed, left the serving tray on the side table, and left the room again. Joel said, "I'm surprised to see you, Jewels. I haven't returned any of your calls for a long time. I thought we had an understanding of no strings attached." He downed his drink and sat the empty glass on the tray. "So what brings you here to the plantation?"

"Oh Joel, is that any way to be?" She moved and placed a hand on his chest. "We were good together once."

He removed her hand and stepped away, staring at her in disbelief. "Jewels, I've moved on with my life, and you should do the same."

"Well." She pulled out her handkerchief, dabbing her dry green eyes. "I read the paper and saw on TV that your parents passed. I went to the hospital, where they informed me you made a permanent move. After checking in at your high-riser, I flew here thinking you might need some Northern comfort."

Joel moved again and placed a hand in his slacks pocket. His voice boomed out, "Listen. What we had was not worthy of you coming here. If I've not made myself clear, Jewels, listen up—I'm not interested in anything with you or from you."

A rap hit the door and Felicite entered with a smile that deepened, charm oozing from him. "Sorry, Joel, but the construction person is here."

"Don't be sorry. We're done in here, right, Ms. Romany?" His blue eyes were the color of steel.

"Oh, we're done, all right, Dr. Wright, more than done." She picked up his glass and aimed to throw it.

Felicite reach for the glass and sat it down, chuckling. "Ah, Ms. Jewels, if you're single and free and perhaps in need of a male escort or companionship while you are here visiting"—he slid a hand down her right arm and stepped closer—"I'm available. Just come to the stable, my office is in there." He straightened his shoulders and walked from the drawing room on out the door, passing Joel and tipping his hat with a huge grin.

Lolita waited on the other woman and said, "Ms. Romany, I'll walk you to your suite."

"Are you a guest?"

Lolita nodded and swayed in her dress walking down the long hallway. "I was a close friend of Dr. Wright's mother—actually I was her companion, and a dear soul."

"So do you and Joel have something happening?"

At Jewels's door, Lolita said in whisper, "A lady never tells!" She whisked down the hall with hands behind her back, smiling like the cat that swallowed the canary. Then she thought, *Only the fact that nothing is going on between that fine doctor and myself.* She ran into the chest of Felicite and bounced off. She was dizzy.

His hands reached out and steadied her by the shoulders. "Walk much?" As he smiled, it became contagious. "Ah, chérie, you were so deep in thought. What's got into you…It's Joel, isn't it?"

Tears slipped and she hung her head. She whispered, "I like him a lot."

Joel rounded the corner and saw the two standing way too close. He fisted his hands. "Lolita, I said not to worry about the room flooding. It's been restored."

Felicite's head jerked and his eyebrows arched. Joel took her hand and left Felicite standing there. Joel said, "I hear there's a fish fry happening in town tomorrow evening in my honor. The Mississippi Community Baptist Church, where my mother played piano, is the host. Lolita, would you attend this event with me?"

"What about your other visiting lady friend, Ms. Romany?"

"Felicite shared his interested in her." He patted Lolita's hand. "It was nice Jewels took the time to travel here. She wanted to offer her personal condolences on behalf of my parents' deaths. Some of us Northerners have manners and do show respect." Joel knew he was stretching Jewels's intent, but it was nice to feel Lolita's hand tighten in his. At her suite's doorway, he bowed and said, "Until tomorrow."

She touched his face and said, "I would like to attend the fish fry with you. What time should I be ready?"

He smiled and placed his hands behind his back to keep from holding her. The attraction to her was growing. "The notice said the festival begins at three. Will that work for you?"

"I'll be ready." She darted into the room, and he heard the door lock.

He thought, *Just maybe this attraction isn't one-sided.*

The next morning at the stables, Joel saw a swollen-lipped Jewels leave his cousin's office in a hurry. He ducked into a stall. Moments later, Felicite opened his office door and stretched his masculine arms in the air.

"Hello, Felicite. I see you had a visitor, and no, she didn't see me."

Felicite scrubbed his face. "Joel, are you sure you don't have any feeling for Ms. Romany?"

Joel's blue eyes twinkled and he said, "Like that matters now!" and laughed.

Felicite frowned. "I want you to know right now that nothing happened between us except a stolen kiss or two. I'm an honorable man when it comes to family and good friends, no?" He placed his feet apart, hands on narrow hips. "Besides, I care too much about her for me to be used if she has any leftover feelings for you. Any other woman and I'd say, use me, but not her, and those green, green eyes."

Joel bunched his lips then said, "Yesterday, I thought I made myself clear. Jewels is a very beautiful, intelligent, caring woman, but we were never meant for each other. To be quite honest, we occasionally hooked up, but neither one of us ever stayed overnight at the other's place. Felicite, don't breathe a word of this to her or anyone else. This is for your ears only. The last few times I was in Columbus, she left messages that she would be in town, but I never responded back. I've moved on." He rambled on, "Now that I've met Lolita, I haven't had the same interest or desire in any other woman." Joel realized what he had said out loud. "Felicite, I've asked Lolita to the fish fry and she has accepted. Take Ms. Romany or whoever else is at your disposal. But to make certain, your friendship with Lolita is just that, isn't it?"

Felicite nodded, and shook hands with his cousin as if concluding a great business deal. Both were now smiling. Then he said, "Let's look at our foal and mother." Side-by-side they walked over to Clare May's stall. Felicite dropped the vitamins in the water and asked Joel to bring in the feed bucket. They mucked the stall and spread hay. The little newborn filly seemed very frisky. They rubbed down the mother and patted the foal. They moved on to the other stalls and ended up at the Appaloosa's. Felicite placed a lead on the colt's halter and slowly walked the colt outside. He walked with him and introduced a blanket to his back. The colt kicked at the ground and his nostrils flared, but he kept walking.

Joel waved and turned in a different direction to meet up with the construction crew. At two o'clock he headed to his suite and bathed. After a long hot shower and shave he was ready to try on the new clothes purchased when he went shopping with Felicite. He was glad he had been breaking in the new leather cowboy boots. He slipped on his choker and glanced in the mirror. His blond hair was collar-length and he could see the resemblance with his cousin. They were more like twins, not identical but nevertheless similar in height and build and, now, in tan. He shook his head and chuckled. Long-sleeved white dress shirt with black piping, black Levis, black tooled cowboy boots, and a black Stetson hat, then Joel graced the stairway. He called to the butler and asked if the horse and buggy were waiting for him out front. Joel sauntered down to Lolita's room. He knocked on her door. She answered, and he took a step backward. Lolita was wearing red cowgirl boots, a short denim pencil skirt, and a low-scoop plaid peasant top filled out at all the right spots. He managed a "Hello. My, look at you…" and smiled. He offered his arm, and together they walked out to the buggy. After helping her onto the seat, he lowered his hat, shielding his eyes. Joel placed a blanket across their laps to cover his unexpected arousal. Her skin glistened and was so creamy, begging to be touched. Lolita smelt heavenly, of orange spice and yet a flora, something sweet. He mentioned her colt and let her speak all the way into town. He nodded from time to time. A trait he learned from Felicite.

He parked the buggy and helped Lolita down. Joel was recognized at once. A huge banner with his professional title—"Dr. Joel Taylor Wright"—hung high in the middle of town. People shook hands and babbled welcome and cheered. He used every inch of charm he could muster. He kissed hands, held babies, patted shoulders, bowed, and smiled until his cheeks ached. The town's committee board had him on stage and made a speech about his mother and her contributions and asked him to join their one and only church in town, the Mississippi Community Baptist, and gave him a key to the city.

Felicite gave a wolf whistle, and then the dancing and the street games began. Joel won a teddy bear for tossing rings over the bottles and gave it to Lolita. He tried his hand at darts and handed Lolita another outlandish oversize stuff dog. She squealed and clapped for his success. He was at the toss-for-a-fish when she grabbed his sleeve. "No more souvenirs…please."

Joel handed his toss balls to a lad behind him and said, "Good luck."

Joel was pumped and had a swagger in his steps. He said, "Are we ready to eat?"

She nodded and moved the stuff animals around to see his face.

He asked, smiling, "Want me to help carry your load?"

Lolita handed him the big floppy dog. They walked over to the buggy and he placed the prize selections on the seat. He reached for her hand and warm sparks traveled through his body. He glanced down at her; Lolita was so beautiful. Her brown eyes were dazzling. She said, "There's the fish fry. I'm starved."

After two large fish sandwiches and a bowl of buttery rich grits Joel said, "Dancing would be nice." He patted his middle. "I need to work off the calories."

She rolled her eyes and grabbed his hand. "Let's do-si-do."

His blue eyes widened, but the music had changed as they stepped onto the floor. It was line dancing, which he had never done. Felicite bumped into him along with Jewels. "Follow me, cousin."

Joel watched and moved his feet and made several wrong turns, but soon he caught on. Clapping and laughing was in the air. The selection of music changed over to a waltz. That he could do with his eyes closed. His upbringing made sure of his dance knowledge. He reached for Lolita's hand and waltzed her on the floor. He pulled her closer as the music again changed. Joel glanced over at Felicite, who held Jewels tight, just swaying. He knew Felicite was trained abroad and dance would have also been a must per Joel's mother. Although, watching Jewels, she didn't seem to mind. He made a turn with Lolita and a dip; he winked and his smile deepened. Jewels reached for Joel's arm. He almost tripped and played it off. Not wanting to make a scene, he let go of Lolita and offered his arm to Jewels. They graced the dance floor, doing a proper waltz. She said, "Thanks for understanding and releasing me from you. I somehow instantly have feelings for your cousin. Maybe, for the first time, true ones. I hope that's all right." She tilted her head upward and smiled.

"I'm down with that. But be gentle with him. I think he cares for you too." They laughed and twirled.

Jewels said, "I'll be leaving the plantation in the morning. I have a flight to catch."

His eyebrows arched, but not a word was spoken.

Felicite finished the dance with Lolita and neither appeared to be happy. They gave daggering stares at Joel and Jewels. A cell phone rang and Joel said, "I'm sorry, Jewels. But I must take this call." It was the hospital. He whisked her off the floor and took two steps away. And then he felt a nearness when he said, "Hello, this is Dr. Wright."

"This is Francine Bilks." The silver haired nurse. She audibly sighed. "Sorry for the call, but our benefit's personnel, Mr. Bob

Chambers, was involved in a car accident. The ambulance has just arrived at the hospital, and from all signs Bob appears to have had a heart attack. Can you come in and assist us? There was quite a pileup of victims. Bob was driving." Joel stared at his phone and his professional behavior kicked in. There was no need to say anything for she had disconnected, and the phone line was silent. He saw Lolita next to him, and Felicite strolled over with Jewels close at his heels. "Felicite, will you escort the ladies to the plantation when they're ready? I've been summoned to the hospital."

"Sure, I'll do this, but I thought you didn't start work until next week?"

"Truer said. However, Mr. Bob Chambers appears to have suffered a heart attack. And according to Nurse Bilks, there's been a several-car pileup." He bent and brushed Lolita's forehead with his lips. "Had a great time tonight, but this is the life of a doctor, always on call." He turned and left the threesome standing. Joel climbed into the buggy and slapped the horse with the reins and said, "Giddyup." He stopped and motioned to Felicite. He handed him the prized possessions of stuff animals and repeated the slap of reins. Although the hospital wasn't far, every minute counted in life and death. He smiled, seeing there was a designated area for horses and carriages. It was a quaint town in a laid-back state, which didn't mean they were any slackers; by no means. He glanced over where the staff parked and his name had been added. He looped the reins over a rail and placed a call to Felicite.

"Joel, anything wrong?"

I need the horse and buggy picked up and my truck parked in my designated area. The hospital lot is crowded with vehicles. I may be here awhile."

"I and my foreman will tend to the matter, pronto."

Joel was met with the serious look of the silver-haired nurse, and for a second he thought she cracked a smile. She motioned and said, "Dr. Wright, thank God you're here. Every doctor and staff member is with a patient. Your scrubs are hanging in the dressing room."

He darted into the locker area and changed clothes and scrubbed up. The nurse was waiting by the door. Joining her, she took the lead with her rubber-soled shoes squeaking each step of the way. He passed by several waiting rooms. People were pacing, chatting, crying, and some appeared to be praying, but strangely, no one seemed to be blaming anyone else. So much difference from the Northern states. He stopped outside the operating room, rescrubbed his hands, and closed his eyes for a moment. "Help! Give me wisdom for my patient that You may be glorified." He air-dried his hands. He watched as the powder was slipped into the Playtex gloves. Nurse Bilks held them out, and with two snaps he moved into the operating room. Staring at the robust, balding man he had briefly met while in interview. He now appeared weak and in a fragile state. "Hello, I'm Dr. Joel Wright. I see you're in good hands with our staff." He glanced at the man's chart, and the nurse pointed several things out. The man had had two stints administered ten years back to aid against artery blockage. It appeared he had another blockage on the left side. Joel knew this was going to be a tricky surgery. Five hours later, after the balloon was used, the old stints replaced, and a rupture artery repaired, Joel discovered Bob had a slight leakage in his right valve.

Nurse Bilks dabbed his brow and saw that the utensils he used were spot-on. She never wavered. They clicked as though they had been a medical team for years.

Joel saw the loss of blood and ordered plasma. She lifted her eyes, but barked out his request. The man was alive, and hopefully would have a speedy recovery. Dr. Joel slipped off his gloves and made minor medicine adjustments. Then he jotted down notes on Bob's chart. Outside the room, the silver-haired nurse said, "You're as good as they say. I do have a question..." and then she paused.

He nodded.

She began as they walked, "That would be, why request a brain wave test for your patient?"

"Hunch. My father, Dr. Charles Taylor's life was dedicated to the research of the brain and its function." He glanced her way. "It was something I remember reading in his study before I shipped his life's work to the OSU hospital. The information seemed to apply to our patient here."

She spoke softly, "We're understaffed at the hospital. Doctor, that's you being paged. You're wanted in the ER for stitches, room 3. Patient is a young male teen, right forearm, underneath."

He entered the room and the young teen was crying like a baby. His mother was trying to console him. After further gazing at the jagged, gaping area, liquid stitches were out of the question. He had his nurse cleanse the area and he scrubbed his hands, snapped on the gloves, and began administering several tiny shots around the affected arm to aid in numbing the area. He said, "Tell me, do you work on a farm?"

The boy's eyes brightened and said, "I won't be able to do anything for a while, will I?"

"No, son, afraid not." He saw the mother wince as he continued with the stitches. He poured on an antiseptic then lightly wrapped the arm in gauze and said, "Change the dressing in two days, and check with your family doctor in ten days. You may take over-the-counter Tylenol for pain as needed." He placed a hand on the boy's shoulder. "Kept it dry and clean." Joel left the room and went on to the next patient, one cubicle after another. Listening and aiding, Nurse Bilks had not left his side, matching his hour by hour, still handing him charts. Joel leaned her way, "Say, don't you ever go home?" and found that he was smiling.

"No, not until you've finished with your last patient. As your assigned nurse, I'm yours, forgotten." She opened the door and followed him inside. It was two thirty-five in the morning when things began to settle down. Joel said, "I'm going to check in on our heart patient before I shower. Nurse Bilk, you're not required to tag along unless I'm on rounds. Go home and get some sleep." But she kept walking and stopped at the nurses' station and asked for Mr. Chambers's chart. In his room, Joel and he were talking. Joel noticed Nurse Bilk holding a chart and said, "Thanks?" and smiled. He glanced at the notes and was glad he had recommended a neurosurgeon to take a look. With the surgery performed on the brain, Bob's signs appeared good. Joel placed the chart back at the end of the bed, and bid an almost sleeping patient a goodnight. Outside the room, Joel said, "I'm going to clean up and try for a few winks inside the doctor's corridors."

She said, "I'll order clean scrubs and a lab coat for you. 'Night, Dr. Wright, or shall I say, 'good morning'?" She walked to the house phone and paged an orderly. Joel assumed his clothes would be in the men's locker room, waiting. He was pleasantly surprised to find in his locker not only clean scrubs but a change of his business dress clothes. Felicite had come as promised. After the shower and a much-needed shave, he slipped into his blue briefs and lay on the cot. His eyes slowly closed. He wakened to his name being paged, and a silver-haired nurse stood looking down at his side, tapping a chart. "What are you doing in here?" he said, gathering a blanket.

"Glad you're among the living," never smiling. "You've been asleep for nearly two hours. Your patient Mr. Chambers took a turn for the worse and he is being prepped again for surgery. Read." She thrust the chart at him.

Without further delay, he edged to the cot and said, "I'll meet you out in the hallway."

She pivoted, and within seconds he was fully dressed in scrubs. They paused at the nurses' station and Joel was handed a black coffee. Nurse Bilks guided him automatically down the hall while he read. His patient was back from a series of x-rays in the operating room with given medicines to stabilize him. He had more than one artery blocked. Joel scrubbed his hands and slid them into the powdered gloves that Nurse Francine Bilks offered, and then he masked up. "Hello, Mr. Chambers." He stared down at the groggy man laboring for his breath, and for the first time in Joel's life, he was proud of his God-given skills. He took a moment and glanced upward and mouthed, "Thanks."

10

LOLITA WATCHED AS her date, the doctor, left the fish fry. She understood that with him being a specialty doctor his services were needed at the hospital, but Dr. Wright did not say more than a "Thank you for attending the fish fry" and a kiss on the forehead, like she was a relative. What was that? And he neither showed further interest nor encouragement to her. She had plans to leave the plantation the next day just like Jewels, but Lolita really didn't want to, so very late in the night she reached her mother by phone. "How are you, Mother?"

"Lolita, what are you doing calling this late? Everything all right?"

"Yes. I'm enjoying my colt and I hate to leave."

Her mother insisted that Lolita stay longer at the plantation and take time to relax and enjoy her new colt.

However, the next evening in the drawing room, Felicite waited until all the servants had left the room and then sternly stated, "Lolita, about Joel Taylor Wright, he is a changed man. The great Northerner's dedication to the South is not in his medical ways but in his own physical contributions." Felicite mentioned the cattle drive he couldn't be on because of being in New York looking for her colt, and how Joel pitched in without complaint and helped his foreman in the roundup of the whiteface cattle and placing them in a holding pen for the auction market. "Joel worked also in transferring other cattle from one field to another without help from me." He held his drink up and sipped. The hour was late in the evening. Felicite held her stare and ordered Lolita out to the barn the next day.

At five the next morning, she joined him in mucking out the stalls, and watering and feeding the horses. They washed up and ate breakfast, then both went back to the barn and spent time with Clare May and her new filly named Daisy, then with Lolita's awesome colt.

Felicite brought out two riding horses, reached for her arm, and said, "Mount up!" They rode a far piece, and then he pointed out the old cabins, explaining that two cabins were already completed. They walked through the other eight. Smiling, Felicite said, "Joel's planning on having resort/retreat here on the plantation and wants advertizing to bring the city and upper-state folk out here for a time of relaxation and to enjoy real country living." He scooted his hat backward. "I just don't know when he'll hire a designer to finish the arty stuff and add furniture to the remaining eight cabins." Eyeing her, Felicite said, "The cabins will be finished next week." Walking back to mount the horses, Felicite turned her way. "Joel needs a website and a designer to display his vision, and a scheduler for the website's call-in clients."

She shifted. "Does he have anyone in mind?"

"What about you?" Felicite eyed her. "Joel intends on offering horse riding lessons, and cultivating riding trails, having campout nights, songs under the stars, perhaps add a fishing time, a fish fry, maybe a yearly rodeo."

A few minutes later she said, "Dr. Wright will be too busy at the hospital to be permanently counted on. You saw what happened at the fish fry event, and he still hasn't made it home yet. You're right, it would take a whole hand of people, from cooks to trail blazers, and event hosts to equipment…and, like you said, there's the website to design and get up and running."

At the barn they handed their reins over to a stable hand, and Felicite nodded and walked into his office.

After dinner, Lolita called her mother for her daily update report. Lynen still insisted Lolita not come home, saying, "The housekeep and staff are more than capable in running the B & B, and, sweetheart, you need a sabbatical for yourself." She insisted that the "good ole Dr. Bennett," who cared for her at the hospital, came by to see her every other day and that he called her twice a day when he couldn't be there. As her mother rattled on, Lolita heard happiness in her voice. Her mother even sounded a little enchanted with having a suitor. Something she had never witnessed before.

That night, Lolita couldn't sleep for she kept thinking about that plantation's doctor. She reached for her sketchbook and began drawing. By midmorning, she had ideas for the furniture decor and what the wall hangings should be in each cabin. After a light lunch, Lolita visited with her colt and led him around the rink, whispering to him, and watched when a patient Felicite introduced a blanket to Chyboon. Felicite was gentle but firm in his handling. They ran their circles, then slowed, and then began again. Lolita made an audible sigh; Chyboon was definitely a beautiful animal, with his tail out and his head forward as he galloping across the rink. Chyboon's spotting was everything and more than she had desired. "Chyboon is so marvelous and strong."

"That he is, and think, Lolita, of all his future foals." Felicite pushed back his Stetson.

"How long before I can ride him?"

Felicite soothingly said, "Several months yet, before we have any built trust in him." Just then the colt whinnied and nicked at his shirt. Felicite whispered in his ears, handing him apple pieces, and the colt's ears turned in. He patted the colt and turned him loose in the designated area while Felicite went on about his daily work. In the stall, he removed his shirt and began the routine mucking. Felicite looked up, "Where are you off to in a huff?" Shaking his head, he returned back to the work at hand.

Lolita yelled over her shoulder, "I've an idea to help out Dr. Wright." She drove her jeep over to the next town and her brown eyes lit up when she spotted the old antique shop. It was open. The wrinkled old man was bustling among the counters when the overhead bell dinged. "Hello."

His smile edged to the warmth in his amber eyes. "Ma'am, what bring you to the Use It Twice Shop?"

Lolita used her cell phone in hand to scroll through her notes and asked, "Do you have any old metal beds or collective dressers? I'm also in need of a few straight chairs, but comfy."

With cloth in midair he said, "What's ya furnishing?"

"Dr. Wright—Joel's his first name—he has restructured and modernized the cabins that were built years ago on his plantation. And two of his cabins are completed and finely decked out. And with him being a doctor and all"—her hands rose, she continued—"he's not able to shop for further cabin needs. He has some crazy hours over there at the hospital."

"Is the doctor Mrs. Elena Wright Taylor's son?"

"He is." She picked up a knickknack and reached for a basket.

"His momma played piano at the church. Such a lovely woman, and a tragedy when we lost her. If this Dr. Wright is anything like his mother, God rest her soul, he's a fine man. Here, walk with me to the back. Beds and dressers are there."

Lolita lost track of time. She tagged seven sofas, a love seat, eight different old chairs, and six dressers. Just then, the shop's bell dinged. She added a few picture frames to her basket, several throw pillows, and tagged ten lamps. She all but squealed. She touched the phone screen, took a deep breath, and placed a call in to the doctor. Five rings and no pick-up. She left a message: "Sorry you couldn't be with me on this adventure, but don't you worry. Felicite shared your cabin's vision, lovely idea, so I made my time available and I am helping you out. See you when your duty allows. Lolita." She felt a smile; inhaled and let it out slowly. She pocketed the cell phone and continued picking up items and whatnots and tagged a few mirrors before coming to the counter. She quietly waited as another customer was delivering furniture. She spotted two more leather sofas and couldn't wait to tag them.

Lolita made a mental note to shop in Jackson for bedding and bed pillows, kitchenette and bathroom towels, supplies, toiletries. She was next in line. "Sir, I tagged merchandise throughout the store and I have this basket filled with treasures. I would also like to tag the other two sofas that were just brought in. Will you hold these until I can get the doctor's credit card? He was called in to the hospital and hasn't made it back to the plantation in two weeks."

"How are you connected to the doctor?"

Lolita thought of the wonderful carriage ride, his desirable kisses, and the way Joel held her while dancing, but she said, "I'm his interior decorator, Lolita Aime." She folded her hands and smiled. She crossed her fingers, for Joel hadn't officially hired or appointed her as anything, but he would.

The older man said, "Ma'am, we'll run a tab for the doctor." He began ringing everything up. He glanced in her direction. "My helper that delivers is one of the fellows who were in that pileup of cars. Although it's his arm and he's healing fine, he still can't lift. Don't suppose you know anyone who would help ya out?" His gray brows lifted.

She pulled out her cell phone and called Felicite. No answer. She clucked her tongue for a second and hung up and spoke to the shop's owner. "I may have the help needed, but can my purchases stay here for a few days?"

The man nodded and reached forward with his wrinkled hand. "Here, miss, is my business card with the shop's hours and phone number." Then he handed her the sales receipt with the itemized list.

Lolita shuffled several large bags and stuffed the information in her purse. He opened the shop door and her jeep. She loaded the bags and thanked the owner. "I'll be back the first of the week, but I'll call first." She smiled and started the engine. Down the road she traveled and made a right turn at the next curve. She drove to Jackson and shopped for bedding and accessories for the cabins, towels, washcloths, and cleaning supplies. She made another call to Joel and again it went straight to voice mail. "Don't you ever answer your phone, this is Lolita! Well, there's no need to shop for things for the cabins." Beep. "Oh that man."

As Lolita drove in, she spotted Felicite. He was walking up the yard. She waved. "Come help me." She jumped down from the jeep and began handing him packages.

"What's this for?"

"The cabins. You suggested I come aboard and use my talent."

"Does Joel know and is he okay with your design?" Shaking his head.

She placed her hands on her curvy hips and said, "I called him and left two voice messages. Now let's take the bags to the first cabin and set everything down in there. Oh, by the way, I need you and your truck and another strong-armed man to do a furniture pick-up next week. You might need to make two trips."

"Does Joel know about this?"

"Sure he does. I told you I left him two voice messages. And my reasoning in asking you is when Joel does arrive back here he'll want to sleep like there is no tomorrow." She carried sack after sack, alongside Felicite's piled-high arms of packages, to the cabin.

"Have you heard from our doctor?"

"Just the once, when he asked me to drop off a change of clothes and his truck, and when I arrived at the hospital I saw every available care-person running toward the ER. That pileup must have been something." He walked back to the plantation's house with Lolita and there they ate dinner. Neither one had an after-dinner drink but went their own ways.

Over the next two days, Lolita took pictures of birds, trees, ponds, cattle, horses, and cotton or sugarcane fields. After the pictures were developed, she matted and framed them. She was so excited to show Joel. However, it was into the third week and still not any word or sight of him. Lolita arranged a meeting with Felicite. After dinner, they went into the drawing room where Lolita presented a website layout of the new "J. W. & F. T Resort/Retreat." The home page featured a weathered log cabin surrounded by fenced-in whiteface beef cattle and riding horses. Next page was a blog on the plantation's resort/retreat, listing the date the plantation was founded and when it had been sold to Elena Wright, and information about the doctor, Joel Taylor Wright, and his cousin, Felicite Tomas, along with their pictures. Underneath the photo tab was added information of the reconstructed log cabins and each one's name. Next tab page contained photographs of a single one-room cabin, a one-bedroom cabin, and a two-bedroom cabin with complete package pricing for an overnight stay, a weekend stay, or a weekly stay. Next tab page was for registration, callback or e-mail with availability and time for the resort/retreat. Last tab page was designed for comments of the guests after their stay. "Well, what do you think?" Lolita clasped her hands in front of her and swayed back and forth.

Just then Joel entered the drawing room. "Hey, you two, what are you discussing?"

Felicite stood and clapped him on the back. "Nice to have you back, although I've enjoyed the quiet while you were out." He chuckled.

"Yeah, yeah, I hear you! By the way, thank you for the clothes and for bringing my truck to the hospital." He glanced at Lolita and said, "I received your messages." He ran his hand through his blond hair. "But I'm a little confused as to what they meant."

Lolita reached for his hand and said, "Felicite explained your idea on a resort/retreat here on the plantation and indicated you needed my help with the design and styling the cabins and in planning the events, so I called you and explained I would take the position. You know my background is in design, art, and photography. Now come take a look." She powered up the computer and was in high spirits.

Joel paled, and not from working all those long hours at the hospital, but from his mind running through the left messages of this woman and her now jubilant explanations and seeing her sparkly brown eyes. He glanced at Felicite standing there and watched him shrug his shoulders. Felicite turned to the computer and said, "Cousin, your input is needed."

Joel's eyes widened as he watched Lolita flip through the website. Her smile was contagious. He felt a pull to her like a magnet. He leaned in over her shoulder and it was all he could do not to touch her. Sleep was the last thing on his mind.

Felicite said, "The last cabin will be finished with its drywall tomorrow. If you're not working, perhaps you can take a look."

He straightened and smiled. "Felicite, I like the idea we're a team in this." He noticed cabin designs lying on the table and picked them up. "Who's the artist?"

Blushing Lolita stood and pointed to the signature. "I am."

Joel sat down and fingered each photograph. "You have a good eye. What's the art plan?"

Lolita brushed his fingers as she pointed. "Some will hang on the cabin walls while the others I will use in our rotating photos on the website."

He stood and went to pour himself a glass of water, but the servant stepped forward and presented Joel with a filled glass. He tasted the water; it was cold and refreshing going down. "Thank you."

Felicite's cell phone jingled. "This is Felicite. You are? Sure thing?" He motioned to Joel and Lolita as he left the drawing room.

Lolita, on tiptoes, kissed Joel lightly on the lips. He brought her closer and thought, *Maybe she can hear my heart pounding.* He glanced down and saw her beckoning, warm brown eyes, and he didn't resist. The kiss was light and then it intensified. He didn't know how long they had locked lips, but when they broke for air they were both gasping. Joel tried to move, but her fingers tightened in his hair. He was definitely attracted to her in more ways than one. He softly said her name.

Lolita shivered, for in that smooth, deep voice, thrills of excitement pulsed through her. She breathed, "Joel," sultry and sweet, just for him.

Both were paused in time, neither one moving. Felicite entered the door and stood staring in, wondering, *Should I leave?*

Joel detected him and said, "Anything important on that call?"

He cleared his throat. "It was the New York Appaloosa breeder's farm. They have bred mares and several six-year-old American fillies for sale. They asked if I would be interested. Seems the owner has taken seriously ill and his wife wants to downsize." Felicite scrubbed his face.

Joel moved a few steps, distancing from Lolita, facing Felicite. "We could use the extra horses for our new adventure and yours on the plantation?" With eyebrows arched he turned back to Lolita. "Change the name of the resort/retreat business to 'J. F. Jackson Resorts.' It has a nice flow, right?" He quickly pointed to the screen and addressed Lolita. "How about changing the green grass to more of a sandy, earthy look?"

"Perhaps add new photos of the horses." Felicite nodded. His cell phone rang again. He glanced at the screen and said, "I'll meet up with you all later." Leaving the room with the phone held by his shoulder, said, "Jewels?"

Joel and Lolita worked for another hour on the website. It was late and Joel tried to suppress yet another yawn. Lolita rolled her neck and placed a hand on it. Joel's eyes followed her hand and he began massaging her neck and shoulders. She went limp and shivered.

Lolita reached for his hand and said, "You have great hands." She stood, and he leaned in and kissed her, running his hands slowly up and down her arms. He was hot, and it wasn't from the balmy weather. He stepped back and jammed his hand in his pockets. Lolita said, "There's an attraction between us and it is growing." She fiddled with her dress's skirt. "Just so you know"—Lolita bit her bottom lip—"I won't have a fling or a one-night stand." For some reason, the words poured from her mouth. "I was in a three-year relationship and I thought it would lead to marriage, but it never happened and I finally realized I never really was in love with him. Your mother offered me to become her companion, and the offer came at a great time. She was a wonderful listener. She advised me to follow my heart, not my mind." She moved a little closer to the door. "Sorry, Joel, if you thought I was possibly leading you on. I know you're an experienced man and also you're a gentleman. Let's remain in the 'Friends Zone.'" She was almost out the door when she added, "See you at the cabins tomorrow," and whisked down the hall and up the stairs toward her bedroom.

He heard the door slam. He moved two steps then stopped. Joel forced himself to finish the glass of water, and carefully set it down. He rocked on his heels then step by step walked toward his suite.

11

The next morning, Felicite caught up with Joel and said, "The cattle are scheduled for market next week. Joel, can your agenda be arranged to help me out?" Felicite looked around. "We have two thousand heads going to auction."

Joel blinked and hastily said, "Sure. I'm looking forward to the auction. I've never been to one."

"Something you won't forget. And from the cattle sale I intend to buy a whiteface bull, hay, and we'll need grain for the year," Felicite said. "Joel, while I'm in upstate New York, our foreman, George, will give you tips on the cattle market and its ways. And thanks, Joel, for your help."

Joel locked eyes with him. "I only hope the horse sale is worth your while."

Just then Felicite's cell phone rang. "See you later, Joel." Felicite hurried away from Joel's hearing. "Jewels, you're calling, why? Was it not in our understanding that if I was interested in a hookup I'd call?"

"Oh Felicite, you know you are, although I'll not be close to the plantation. My stopover is in New York and is scheduled next Tuesday afternoon until Monday morning five o'clock. I really want to see you."

He rolled his brown eyes and wondered how many other men she had said that to. "I will be in New York Tuesday evening. Meet in Central Park." And he thought, *We'll go from there.* "Tuesday at 6:00 pm." Felicite shivered after the phone call disconnected and he wasn't cold. He secretly was excited about their hookup. He rolled his shoulders and made arrangements for his flight into New York, and then went looking for Lolita or Joel. He heard voices and glanced toward the cabins. Joel's hands were flapping in the air like a giant bird. Lolita had her hands on her hips and then pointed a finger at Joel's chest. He began backing up. Felicite cleared his throat. "Knock it off, you two!" He locked eyes with Joel. "So what's your impression on the cabins?" He easily smiled and said, "I had the plantation crew continue on the cabins after the new wing was built and completed."

An item on the bed caught Felicite's eye; he reached over and picked up the art piece. "Isn't this one of your mother's favorite pieces that she painted? The crop fields." He glanced over at a gaping Joel.

"Felicite, this cabin project seems like a runaway train." Joel placed his hands on his hips. "Where's my input on the cabin or its structure or in its features or, for that matter, the design?"

He stared at Joel. "Man, your footprints are all over the first cabin. How else would I have known what your expectations were? Are we in this resort/retreat together or were you just blowing wind about an 'us'?" Lifting his sweaty, stained hat, he hit his thigh.

A tear slipped down a pale Lolita's face and, almost in a whisper, she said, "I don't know where our plan went so wrong. You never called me back to say no." She turned to walk away then said, "I've ordered furniture for the other nine cabins, and Felicite has that information." She turned. "Good-bye, Joel, I'm going home!"

Joel caught her arm. "Look, I'm sorry, and just a little surprised and, well, tired. I haven't slept in over forty-eight hours and had very little catnapping before that. Lolita, please stay and continue with your designs, unless, that is, you're needed at the B. & B. Your designs are smartly done." He kept her close.

She felt his breath upon her face and the room swirled.

"Lolita, Lolita." He caught her and, as she opened her eyes, he kissed her then and whispered, "You're driving me crazy."

"Let me down. Now! Who do you think you are that you can kiss me anytime you have a desire and then walk away from me like I'm a cold fish?" Her lips thinned, she said, "Well, am I working for you on the resort/retreat design or not?" Her brown eyes were flashing darts.

Joel glanced over at Felicite and then at Lolita. "Strangely, Felicite, I have heard my mother speak of her painting, and thank you both for adding it to the design. And for coming together and rescuing me on this project. Teamwork is not something I'm used to." He blew out a breath. "Now about the layout for the website—how long, Lolita, before it can be rolled out?" His lips lifted slightly.

Felicite mentioned, "We need employees, a horse trail, a cook, a guide or two, entertainment, a place mapped out for a campout and fire pit, and horses for the experienced and inexperienced riders. All this needs to be completed before any real scheduling of clients can be done."

"All right. This is April, so let's shoot for the weekend of September 1, 2016," said Joel.

Felicite and Lolita nodded and at the same time answered, "September first it is."

Joel in his low voice said, "I'm grateful for you both." He glanced over at Lolita. "Are we all right?" Then, in Felicite's direction: "Want me to drive you to the airport Tuesday?"

"Thanks, but no. I like to get behind the wheel after a flight. It settles me."

Lolita spoke. "Joel, we'll work on us…but right now the furniture from the shop needs pick-up and your signature."

She walked over to tap Felicite on the shoulder. "Are you helping him with the move?"

He shrugged his shoulders. "Call the owner and see if we can come in today, right, Joel?"

"Sure."

A few minutes later, she waved the men off.

Felicite said, "We'll take both trucks. I'll let the foreman know we're leaving so he can gather help for when we get back."

At the antique shop, the owner smiled and pumped both Felicite's and Joel's hands. He said, "Dr. Wright, I would know you anywhere. Your mother—God rest her soul—was a great artist in every way, and is so missed at the church. No one could play the piano keys like she did. What an angel." He finally released Joel's hand. "Your items are tagged throughout the store. Just holler if you need any help."

Joel looked over at Felicite and rolled his blue eyes, but kept smiling. Of course the shop didn't have air-conditioning; the day proved to be a hot one and the sweat poured freely. Both truck beds were filled and piled way too high, and so were the passenger seats, but between Felicite and Joel, they had everything Lolita tagged loaded. Joel paid with credit card to the sum of three thousand twenty-eight dollars and eighty-nine cents, still smiling and nodded to the store owner, until he thought his smile was a permanent fixture.

The trip back to the plantation was slow-going, and Felicite used a lot of back roads. Joel gladly followed. Four and a half hours later, they pulled into the plantation's driveway. Felicite tooted his horn, and the foreman with men came running. They helped carry the furniture to the nine cabins.

Joel noticed each cabin now had its own bed or beds, a dresser with mirror, end table, chair or sofa, and lamp.

Lolita walked along with the men into each room, carrying bag after bag of whatnots, bedding, towels, and added toiletries, placing everything just so. Joel and Felicite made beds, hammered nails in the walls for the artwork or photography as Lolita instructed, and they cleaned out the bathrooms. The three bodies stood side by side, admiring each cabin. Joel began laughing. The others peered at him. He said, "I don't remember a time when I was so dirty or smelly."

Felicite shook his head. "Hang with me mucking stalls or riding herd on the plantation or when it's branding time."

Lolita laughed along with the men and they stopped and glared at her. She only had a dust spot on her right cheek, and she hadn't appeared to have broken in a sweat, and was in a dress at that. "Great job we've done!"

The hour was late and morning would come all too soon. Felicite would be headed to New York and Joel would be making early rounds at the hospital before seeking out George the foreman. Lolita promised she would finish the rollout of the website and begin placing ads for the newly created job positions.

Morning came all too early. Joel dressed in business clothes and ate a hearty breakfast, thanking a beaming Elsa. At the hospital on rounds, wearing his white, flapping coat, he was glad to see his boss sitting up after his surgery and eating on his own. He stopped in for a few words. "Glad you're back among the living, Mr. Chambers."

He chuckled and said, "We did the right thing by hiring you. Thanks, Dr. Joel Taylor Wright, for using your knowledge and know-how." The man continued eating his toast and took a sip of black decaf coffee.

"Mr. Chambers." Joel picked up the chart and scribbled on it. "You may leave the hospital when the nurse arrives with your paperwork, but don't drive until after you have had your next checkup. And you're welcome. Thanks for hiring me so I could share my God-given talent." Both men laughed.

Bob Chambers touched the doctor's sleeve. "When can I return to work?"

Joel pursed his lips. "I'll see you in six weeks for your checkup, unless anything develops sooner, and if everything is good you may return to work the following Monday, but with limited hours. You may want to think on a partner or a full-time benefits personnel and you take a part-time schedule." Joel placed the chart back into its slot and turned to leave, then said, "Mr. Chambers, I would like to make a few contacts in my field and in other areas of doctoring to aid this hospital and to lead it into the twenty-first century. Are you open to other doctors being hired?"

"Son, let me give that some thought, but it wouldn't hurt to inquire—quietly, of course."

With a nod of the head, Joel left the room. He checked in with the staffing and saw he could place himself on a 24/7 call basis and he notified them he would be out of phone range on the two days of cattle market. When he stepped outside the hospital he swung by the local florist and selected a mix bouquet of colorful Gerbera daisies, tulips, and blue roses which reminded him of Lolita, who was beautiful, different, and alluring. He selected a random card, signed it *Just Joel*, and carried the mix bouquet of flowers to the truck. He flipped on his radio and a tune by Toby Keith called "As Good As I Once Was" was playing. It really wasn't his style of music, but the words were catchy and he found himself thumbing on the steering wheel and singing along. He felt even at peace. At the plantation, he turned off the radio and the engine. He headed to the dining hall for it was almost dinnertime. He met Elsa and smiled, pulled out a blue rose and handed it to her. Her dark face turned red and she waved him on. Joel sat at the table and then a fragrant Lolita waltzed in. Joel stood, handed Lolita the bouquet of flowers, then kissed her cheek. His rich voice said, "Thank you for overlooking my poor attitude and for believing in my dream and seeing a future here on the plantation. Your design and photographic work is impeccable." He winked and softly added, "Just like you," and he squeezed her shoulders.

She smelled the blue roses and, admiring, said, "I must place these lovely flowers in water, excuse me."

He stood and watched her sway from the room. His stomach rolled; he was hungry, and for more than a tasty home-cooked meal. She entered again. He stood, she smiled. He said, "Lolita," his heart plummeted to his stomach when she turned to him with the smile broadening and dewy brown eyes sparkling.

She reached over and placed a hand properly on his forearm and the heat penetrated all though his body. He watched her flinch; she felt something too. His want of her intensified. Joel abruptly stood and excused himself from dinner, making a lame excuse. "I have a phone call to make. See you tomorrow." Joel, without another word, straightened and placed his steps one in front of the other, until he was behind not just a closed door but a double-locked door. He did not trust himself at the moment. He jerked off his suit coat and pulled off his tie while, mumbling, "She's not like any of the other women." Joel turned on the cold water and was glad he had the bathrooms upgraded with better water pressure. He shivered and stood a long time under icy waters. After slipping into his jeans and Cranbury shirt, he pulled on his boots, grabbed his Stetson hat, and made his way out to the barn. He sat on a hay bale sorting out his mixed-up feelings toward Lolita. He questioned whether he wanted anything out of life, love, children, or to be a family man? He said in a whisper, "And what with my being a ten-nation kind of man?" He placed his head in his hands. "Perhaps someone like Lolita would find me undesirable and unworthy and certainly not…husband material." He jerked himself up as if he had been prodded with an electrical jolt. Was he considering marriage for the first time in his life? Sweat broke out on his forehead, and he felt sick to his stomach, like he had worked outside all day in the heat.

Millions of stars hung in the firmament and the yellowish full moon set low. He inhaled. The air was easy to breathe and he took a country moment to enjoy. Nothing was completely settled in his mind. Maybe someday he could talk with Lolita, or maybe not. Shaking his head and placing on his hat, he thought, *I'd be so vulnerable.* A flashback came to mind, the day he was sent to military boarding school. Desiree had stooped to his short level and held him close and said, "Joel Taylor Wright, you're smart, you're kind, and you're handsome," then his father reached for his small hand and placed it in his and walked him to the waiting car. A tear threatened to fall, but Joel had blown his nose and faced forward in his seat, not looking back as the driver moved on.

He tugged at his hat, pulling it forward, and decided he couldn't risk or handle any rejection from Lolita, because of who he was or wasn't or what genetic or heritage makeup he had come from. She did disapprove of him being a Northerner. Joel let out a sigh and walked to the plantation house kicking at the dried ground and said, "She deserves someone better than me." With that settled in his mind, he would let Lolita know the Friend Zone was all he could ever offer her.

However, any conversation would have to be postponed until another morning. For bright and early, the foreman arranged for rentals of fifty-seven double-decker cattle trailers and their drivers to arrive.

Joel ate a hearty breakfast and scurried from the dining room before Lolita could question him. He joined George and, as clockwork, every half hour several trailers were loaded and moved. Then the next set of trailers arrived and lined up to load more cattle. That scheduling lasted all day and well into the night. It was in the wee hours when the cattle reached the market and were finally placed in their holding pens with hay and water. They would be sold within two days at the private auction for meat packers only.

Both men, George and Joel, bunked in Joel's truck for a few hours of sleep. Joel was awakened to a knock on his window and the smell of roasted coffee. It was George. Joel was amazed how the foreman moved around with grace and ease. Both waited their turn in line at the porta-pot area and Joel was relieved to find it had running water. After washing his hands he splashed his face and slicked back his blond hair, badly in need of a cut, which had grown past his shirt collar and had a wave. He plopped on his hat, pulling it forward, and waited on George the foreman to tell him what to do next.

George motioned. They strode over to the cattle area and spoke to the helper of the pen before the man hopped over the fence. George introduced Joel to the tall, slender, leathered-looking cowboy. He nodded and smiled before the cowboy swung himself upon the saddled horse. Joel stood with amazement at the cowboy's talents, using his lariat and doing a shrill whistle to move fifty head of cattle into the arena and keeping them there for the meat-packing companies to bid on.

George carefully motioned to Joel to watch from the sideline in the bleachers as the bidding took place. He sat with him and pointed out, "The meat-packing companies come from all over the world for our stock. That began with Felicite's father. See, there's United States, Canada, Africa, and Brazil, and there are many more countries represented. You'll need to keep your hands down, don't tip your hat or remove it while the bidding is under way. Now watch the intended bidder as to how they bid."

Joel's eyes widened when the auctioneer began. The man's tongue rolling out the bidding numbers and the spit flew. Hands were raised, heads bobbed, a hand movement across the bill of a hat of this company and that company and then several at the same time. It was hard to keep track of the person that won the bid of the fifty cattle. Joel's eyes followed over to George as he would nod occasionally to the auctioneer to either up the cattle price or stay. Then a wooden hammer sounded and the auctioneer said, "Pen number fifty-two sold." The next grouping of fifty cattle was herded into the arena with the cowboy easily twirling his lariat, and the auctioneer began again. "Pen number ten, place your bid." The hand gestures, hat touches, and nose twitches, again and again, as the round-bellied man beckoned pricing from the crowd. George nodded again, the hammer pounded, and the man said, "Sold pen ten. Pay the lady ten thousand dollars at the office."

George leaned over toward Joel. "The first head of fifty cattle sold for two hundred dollars each. The second set of cattle sold for the same amount. If the buyers keep buying at this price, Felicite will be able to buy two bulls of his choice and enough feed and hay to last out the reminder of year."

The next set of fifty cattle was in the arena, and bids were steadily being made.

George said, "You do the nod this time when the auctioneer looks your way. Wait, wait, be quick with the head jerk and no smiling. Now!"

Joel did as instructed and the joy filtered through his system as if he had accomplished a great goal. He had to bite the inside of his cheek to not smile.

George elbowed Joel and whispered, "Great job!" He scooted his hat forward and said, "Do you think you can handle the next group of cattle being auctioned off? I may wander over to the food cart and talk with Honey. After the next fifty cattle, the auctioneer will break for thirty minutes, then a replacement auctioneer will continue."

Joel was glad when the break began. He stretched his legs and opted for a bottle of water and a quick turn at the port-a-potty, then entered the arena's bleachers and sat down. The second auctioneer began and continued nonstop until after the fourth pen of cattle for the day was sold. After another short break, George scooted in next to Joel.

Then the first auctioneer announced they were tag-teaming the last two cattle pens for the evening bids. The hammer pounded. The meat-packing representatives were ready. At the closing, an announcement was made. "Another thousand head of cattle for bidding will begin bright and early in the morning, five o'clock."

The next day was more of the same, and the sale of the cattle was not disappointing. The amount of $10,000.00 per fifty heads continued. Joel walked along with George to pick up the plantation's check of $40,000.00 dollars at the makeshift office. They grabbed a bite to eat and both ordered a large black coffee to go. It was a successful profiting; two long days, but Joel swung behind the wheel of his truck, happily. George buckled up and turned toward Joel. "You did well yesterday and today, like a real cowboy."

12

FELICITE PARKED HIS trucked and hurried inside the airport to catch his flight in to New York. He found the flight was smooth and arrived early. Felicite hailed a cab and headed toward Central Park. He decided to splurge. He booked himself into an upscale hotel instead of staying in a motel on the outer edge of town. This way he could be closer to the events and activities of the city.

Felicite was more relaxed this time away from the plantation for he knew he could depend on Joel and that George would guide him. Then he chuckled. So would Lolita.

Felicite's thoughts returned to Jewels. He considered asking her about a monogamy commitment to him. He smiled. Felicite would like to court her properly, but he needed to call Joel just to be certain that he was cool with him and her possibly being an item. He didn't want to break any man code.

Felicite checked into the J. W. Marriott Essex House, New York, and was satisfied with the pricing of $293.00 dollars per night. For New York, the hotel room was spacious and clean. It even had two comfortable sitting chairs and a round table. The bathroom was sizeable and he liked the rain showerhead. Felicite hung his long-sleeved shirts and dress jeans with belt in the armoire and unpacked his lounge clothes, socks, underwear, and T-shirts, placing them in the dresser. He bounced on the king-sized bed and sank down into it saying, "Yeah, this is living." He thought that maybe Joel and his ways as the Northerner could rub off on him a little.

Felicite call Joel. Third ring.

"Dr. Joel Taylor Wright here."

"Joel, it's me, Felicite. I need to run something by you again, but first tell me how the market went."

"Hey, Felicite, I take it you made your flight all right. And the auction from beginning to end was quite the lesson to me. Actually, it was intriguing, and George showed me how to accept bids when they were made. He's one of a kind, a keeper, I'd say."

"You bet he is. Maybe we ought to think about him having his own bungalow on the plantation. I'm sure he'll want to settle down someday and having a bunk in the bunkhouse. I'd sure hate to lose our foreman."

"Felicite, why don't you consider moving into the west wing in the plantation house? I'm moving into the east wing today, and Lolita is helping decorate. Or for that matter there's the north wing or the south wing. It's not like we don't have room."

"Great idea. I'll take the west wing. That was a great idea to have all four wings with back entrances. So will the north and south wings of the house be for our personal guests?"

"That was my idea."

"Awesome. But, Joel, seriously I need to ask you"—clearing his throat—"I know you said that Jewels was a passing ship that sailed, but how would you really feel if I pursued her, and not as a hookup? You there?"

Joel muffled a laugh. "Felicite, you mean like bringing her out to the plantation sometime to stay? Man, are you serious?" A long pause.

"I am, Joel. I...I can't seem to wash her out of my system. I'm to meet up with her tonight."

"That's major. To tell you the truth, we never had that great of a connection, and settling down never entered my mind. She's a good woman and would be loyal. If she's the one you want to lasso, go for it. I'm more than okay if she were to be around. We were over before it ever began." His voice trailed off. "I'm having my own issues and thoughts about someone." Then the phone lines were disconnected.

Felicite saw the time was quarter until 5:00 p.m. He jumped into the shower, and by five after five, he headed for the elevator, pausing long enough to make a reservation at a restaurant across the street. He placed his cell phone away, shaking his head, thinking, *Money can by almost anything.* He lowered his black Stetson and continued his walk in the park, looking for Jewels. He hadn't realized the acreage was so extensive. He stood with legs apart and viewed the land, taking in the variety of flowers, and heard the sound of running water. Someone touched his arm. He inhaled; it was Jewels, and his breath was knocked out of him. She was past beautiful. She was breathtaking. Was his tongue hanging out? He moved his hand over hers and in his gravelly voice said, "Nice to see you again, ma'am."

She giggled and scooted closer. "Cowboy, I've been counting down the hours until we met again."

Her sweetness wreaked havoc all over his body; he was on high alert. He said, "Have you eaten?"

She shook her head no and her smile grew. He said, "I made reservations earlier. Would you care to dine with me?" He held his breath.

She laced her hand in his and said, "Cowboy, lead the way," and gave his fingers a squeeze.

How he kept on walking and appeared not affected, he didn't know. She was sizzling hot in her pencil skirt and off-shoulder blue top. Her bare shoulder was so white and begged him to touch. They were seated across from each other in a secluded area in the restaurant. He asked what she would like to drink; Felicite wanted something strong, but coffee was his limit with her around. She asked for a glass of Chardonnay. The waiter in white gloves moved gracefully and quietly away from them. She asked, "So what brought you to New York?"

He glanced into her green eyes and was lost for a second. Felicite removed his hat and placed it on a seat beside him. He hated how thick his wavy red hair fell forward. He said, "We, Joel and I, have decided to use part of the plantation for a resort/ retreat, a getaway for the city folk. And we'll need more horses. A while back, I bought a colt and a bred mare in New York, and I'm pleased. They notified me of their stock sale and I thought I'd take a look." He lifted his coffee cup and noticed only a part of her wine was left.

The waiter came. Felicite ordered steak and vegetables and she ordered soup and a house salad. Their hands touched over the bread basket. An electric volt traveled all through his body. She quickly removed her hand and placed them in her lap. How was he to eat with her so close?

Jewels said, "I had a pony when I was ten years old and learned how to ride. And later my father bought me a pinto horse. 'Ole Spree,' I called him. I really don't know why, but the name just suited him." She reached for a roll, continuing, "He was old when my father died and the people who bought the farm wrote him into their contract. They had a young girl who seemed to have taken to Ole Spree."

"What about your mother? Didn't she want the farm?"

She sipped from the wine glass and set it down. "I don't remember my mother. I was told she left my father when I was just two years old. I don't know where or why she left. It was just dad and me while growing up, and I used the money from the sale of the farm, wisely, and went to airline schooling and became a flight steward. That way I could travel the world and meet interesting people." She smiled.

"Jewels…" The food arrived and all conversation was tabled. After their plates were removed and dessert was ordered to share, he leaned in. "I'm sorry that you never knew your mother." They sat there, gazing at each other, and Felicite felt at ease. So he told her the story of his mother's death and how she was the love of his father's life. And how Joel and he were related. After Felicite paid the bill and left a hefty tip, he asked, "Where are you staying?" He noticed in the street light, she was blushing.

Jewels said, "I haven't a room."

Once again they stopped in the middle of the street. He pulled her near and placed his arms around her and bent down. His breath went ragged. "Jewels, I'm nuts about you. I want more than a, well, a romp in the hay." His eyebrows lifted. "Jewels, would you ever consider marrying a man like me?"

She touched his lips with her finger. "Are you asking me to be your wife? We really don't know that much about each other." Her green eyes widened. And people were bumping into them.

Felicite swung her around and said, "Darling, I am. Will you marry me? I'll love you forever." Then he went in for a long-over-due kiss.

She placed a hand on his chest. Someone yelled, "Get a room!"

He only held her tighter. "Felicite, I will marry you, but you must understand I don't believe in divorce, and I'm scared. This is all happening way too fast."

He watched her as he said, "I knew you were the one the night I was introduced to you at the plantation." Jewels began to speak, but he shook his head. "The past is behind us and God does work in mysterious ways." Felicite squeezed her arm. "Where's your overnight bag? And how much notice does the airline need that you've quit? We'll marry day after tomorrow and our life will be a full-time journey!"

She realized it was a statement. He wasn't asking. She smiled and thought, *It's nice once in a while for a man to be a man. And what a handsome cowboy.* They went to the airport and she withdrew her baggage from a locker and he hailed a cab back to his hotel. Felicite kissed her several times in the elevator and said, "You'll sleep in the bed. I'm taking the couch." He waved his long finger at her and said, "We are going to wait until we are married. No hookups for me ever again, or for you."

She couldn't stop smiling, but nodded. "But I need to go shopping for a dress, a wedding dress."

He slipped off his coat and placed his hat on the round table, and offered to hang up her wrap. He walked over to the phone and dialed housekeeping. "Please send up a pillow and a blanket to Room 222. Thank you." He turned toward Jewels. "How about while I'm at the horse sale tomorrow you go shopping. Here's my credit card."

From her neck up, she was red. She squealed, "I have some money, but what a kind, gentlemanly act."

He placed the credit card back in his billfold. "In the morning, we'll head over to city hall and apply for our marriage licenses, then grab a bite to eat. Yes?"

"Yes, but are you sure"—patting the bed—"you want to sleep over there tonight?"

"You're driving a hard bargain, but I respect you too much to take advantage of you, even though you are a tempest." He closed the distance between them and showed her in a long, deep kiss how badly his want was for her. There was a knock on the door.

"Housekeeping."

Felicite stepped back and answered the door and handed the woman a tip. He arranged the bedding on the couch, then used the bathroom. He appeared in his lounge bottoms, shirtless, and he watched as her breath caught. He was freshly shaved, bronzed, broad shouldered, and muscular. His arm muscles rippled and his six-packs were to die for.

She traced a hair patch on his solid chest to his waist and gulped for air. He was built like a model and soon he was going to be her man. She gathered her bag and a made quick steps into the bathroom and locked the door. Jewels needed space and cold water to quench the heat from her body. She hadn't known any of his plans and hadn't planned or thought on whether she would be staying over or heading out on another assignment. Now that they had met and he had asked her to marry him, Jewels squealed, "I'm getting married in just two days." She let the bath water run deep. She used oils and bubble soap, slipped out of her clothes and tried to relax. Jewels glanced down at her newly pedicured toenails, and was happy she had made a last-minute decision to have them prepared, and was glad she had packed several lacy undergarments. The water became more than cold. She dried and shimmied into her barely-there baby-doll pajamas. "Crap, no robe." She came from the room and saw her cowboy under the blanket on the couch with his Stetson hat over his face. She dimmed the light and sank her body into the king-sized bed and pulled the covers up, thinking, *I'll never sleep.*

Felicite had a great view of his bride-to-be and her shapely long, white legs.

He didn't mind the back view either. She was well rounded. When Jewels reached to pull up the covers, he got a glimpse of her frontal endowment. He closed his eyes tight and adjusted his lounge bottoms. Two days couldn't come fast enough. He tossed and turned, and by five in the morning Felicite was dressed waiting for the sun to come up and streetlights and honking horns to begin the day. At 7:00 a.m., she awoke. Her hair was chaotic and yet she stole his heart. He had never felt like this about any woman. He wondered how it had happened. Love just flew up and bit him. Jewels slipped from bed and went into the restroom. Half an hour later, she was dressed, hair and makeup completed. "Let's go down and eat."

By 10:00 a.m., they were standing outside at the city hall office of the marriage bureau, waiting to apply for their marriage license. They were squeezing hands, laughing, and eyeing each other with heated intent. Felicite leaned in and nuzzled her porcelain neck and asked, "Will you have to take the flight out of here on Monday?"

She breathed in and held his hands in hers. "No. No more flights or me being a stewardess." With her eyes moist she said, "I only want to be your wife and serve you."

"You do know I put in long hours on the plantation and sometimes I'm out all night. Cattle get out, a calf is born, a mother is lost. And then there's the sugarcane, and the cotton fields. Trust me, I'm not trying to have you change your mind, it's just I can't always be with you, and then there is the new adventure Joel's trying to launch, the resort/retreat."

She touched his lips and said, "But there are times when you'll be free. I'll take that. I love you, Felicite Tomas. I fell for you the first day at the plantation, even before you introduced yourself. Your brown eyes tell a story in themselves." She on tiptoe kissed him.

"Next, number twelve," the lady said as the door stood open at the license bureau.

Felicite checked the slip of paper he was holding; they were number 12. They stepped into the office and filled out forms; then finally, there was the one important form which was now filled out. Felicite wore a broad smile and, gripping Jewels's arm, they waited for the instructions to appear before the judge the next day. He paid the twenty-five dollars and they were on their way. Outside on the street he asked, "So are you going shopping?"

She rolled her eyes and patted his hand. "Catch your cab and be off with your horse business. I'll see you in the morning. Can I have the hotel room's key card?"

He reached into his front shirt pocket and handed her the card. "What do you mean we'll meet up tomorrow? I shouldn't be too late. We can have dinner together when I return."

Jewels shook her head. "No, my love. You can't see me the night before our wedding." She giggled. "Find you another room for the night, cowboy!"

He stood gawking in disbelief, and a laugh bubbled out until it was a complete, heavy belly laugh. Finally he said, "You do know how to bring a man to his knees. Will you at least call me to let me know you're all right?" And he reached for his wallet and slipped her a credit card. "Please honor me. Pay your expenses for the day from me—spa, hair, nails, eating, or whatever a woman does to prepare for her wedding day. I'll miss you!" He kissed her, turned, and walked to flag a cab.

Jewels had never met such a determined man. She pocketed the charge and went shopping for her dress. She wanted an off-white, but wasn't sure on the style. After the fifth store and nowhere near making up her mind, Jewels went for a walk. Several stores she waved off, and there, to the right of where she was standing, was a hole-in-the-wall shop that beckoned her in. She spotted her dream nightwear, and then the dress, which was beachy-looking and oyster-white in color. The fabric was sheer and airy and, to her surprise, cotton. The sleeves came to midlength on the arms; the top was straight across and dipped low in the back. The skirt draped around the hips, then had a sudden flare. The saleswoman showed Jewels a pair of sassy, off-white-and-black thin-strapped heel sandals, and they were a must. She pulled out her card and paid. She walked until she saw a jewelry store and said, "It won't hurt to look." Several hours later, she chose his card to purchase his wedding ring. Closer to the hotel, she located a hair salon and went inside. An hour later, she bustled about carrying the packages and stopped in at a Western men's shop. Jewels asked the salesman, "Do you have any bolo ties? He began walking and slid behind the counter. He lifted a tray and asked, "See any you admire?"

She selected a silver one with a place to add a small picture. She had the salesman snap her picture; she would have it printed and placed in the slot on the bolo tie. The salesman handed her a covered slim box containing the bolo tie and added an unsigned card in the sack. She was a little tired from not sleeping well and was only too happy to hang up her clothes and place his wedding gift next to her purse. Jewels ordered in. She stretched and drew bathwater and slid down, covering her shoulders. She heard the knock on the door and rushed out of the tub. She had lost track of time. She pulled on one of his shirts and his lounge bottoms and answered the door. She ate the soup of the day, chicken noodle, with salad, and sipped on a glass of wine. Jewels was happier than she could ever remember. She lay down for a while, saying, "I'll call Felicite later." She drifted to sleep and jerked to a pounding noise at the door. "Who's there?" she called out shakily.

"It's me, Felicite. Are you all right? I've been worried sick. My cell phone doesn't have any bars left and I hadn't heard from you in this big city."

"I'm sorry, I meant to call, but I fell asleep. It looks like it's still dark out."

"Jewels, its three thirty in the morning. I couldn't stay away not knowing if you were here and safe."

"Oh, sweetheart, I'm fine." She swung the door open, needing to see him as much as he sounded that he needed to see her.

"Jewels, what about us not seeing each other before the wedding?"

"Oh, let's not get caught up in all that traditional stuff. You're here, I'm here."

A broad grin came across his face, and his strong arms reached out for her, and a kiss lingered. Sometime later, they left the room and went for breakfast and talked nonstop about her move to the plantation and how he had just taken over the newly renovated west wing.

Time was ten until 10:00 a.m. Arm-in-arm, they walked into the West Chapel and waited another forty-five minutes to be seen. The ceremony was short and to the point. Not romantic, not spoken with caring words, but with much practiced authority. Jewels was just as pleased as if the wedding had been with all the bells and whistles. She said "I do" when the time was right to accept Felicite as her husband, and she held her breath until they were pronounced "man and wife." She watched his brown eyes change like the color of coal as he kissed her.

The marriage license was signed and the next couple to be married was their witness. Felicite paid the thirty-five dollars and out the door and onto the sidewalk they stood. She handed him a narrow box. She glanced admiringly at the brilliant cut-diamond wedding ring he had just placed on her third finger of her left hand. Jewels smiled and looked up at him. He had the silver bolo tie in his hand and clutched it to his chest. In almost a whisper, Felicite said, "I love you. Thanks for the wonderful gift. I'll wear it on Sundays when we go to church. So thoughtful."

Jewels on tiptoes kissed his cheek, and he bent, catching her cherry lips. He said, "Mrs. Jewels Tomas, let's take a carriage ride around the park."

"My husband, I would like that."

They hugged and kissed, then he hailed the carriage driver.

13

LOLITA ADMIRED THE oversize bright red and organ chair that the antique owner included when the cabin furniture was delivered. She had oohed and ahhed so much that Joel presented her with the chair to place in her remodeled suite. She also appreciated the indoor commode. The plantation suites and wings were the top of the line in decor and modernization; Joel had spared no expense. Lolita was pleased that Joel agreed she should keep the same suite his mother had assigned her as a young adult. Joel encouraged her to use her photographic work in the older rustic design.

Lolita stretched then yawned, and thought, *Joel is a different soul now than when I first met Mr. Northerner.* And said out loud, "Unfortunately, he's kept his word that we should stay in the Friend's Zone." She walked over to the bed, pulling the covers back, said, "Although it's nice to finally talk at ease with him, but I had hoped for so much more. I really don't know when Joel's interest in me changed or why. Those kisses we once shared…I miss them."

It was five in the morning, and Lolita dressed in faded jeans and a cropped blouse knowing the day before her would be laborious. It was her turn to help muck out the old mare's stall and her colt's. She gathered the shovel, pitchfork, and wheelbarrow, and watched as George showed Joel some basic walking and standing procedures used in training her colt.

Lolita caught Joel smiling several times as he groomed the horses. He nodded to her and said, "At 8:00 a.m. I'm expected at the hospital to make my rounds. I'll be gone until dinnertime."

Lolita smiled and went about her chore. She tried to catch glimpses of him tending to horse after horse. She could admire him from a distance. Oh, that man…

Just then, George entered the barn and walked over to Joel. "A call came in for Felicite from the owner of Triple A & G. He's ready to sell Truant, their registered prize-winning bull." George swatted his straw hat. "Felicite has to respond within the next twenty-four hours or the owner will move on to the next person interested. Joel, that time runs out today at 11:00 a.m.! I've tried calling Felicite, but his cell phone rolls over to voice message. What are we to do?" George extended his hands upward.

"How much is the asking price for Truant?" Joel ran a hand through his still-longer blond hair.

Lolita came near to the men, but kept silent.

"He's asking eighteen thousand dollars. Felicite budgeted fifteen thousand for the bull and he won't be happy at the price increase," George said.

"Thanks for coming and speaking to me about this matter." He slapped George on the back and said, "I'll call the owner about the bull. What's the number?"

George's small black eyes narrowed, but he said, "Let's step over to Felicite's office and I'll get you the number."

Lolita waited outside the door of the office and caught Joel's arm when he stepped out. "I know Old Man Lenard from A & G. You'd do better bargaining with him in person than over the phone." Lolita paused, bunching her lips "You're a Northerner." She gazed into his fiery blue eyes and said, "Call him and set up a time to meet with him. His farm is in Alabama. I could go with you and perhaps ease any friction that may surface."

Joel searched her brown eyes and said, "You'd do that for me?"

She batted her long eyelashes and said, "Let me know when." She walked toward the old mare's empty stall and began spreading the straw, and turned to a still-staring Joel. "What?" Lolita placed her hands on her hips.

Joel shook his head and walked past her into the yard, pulled off his shirt, and patted the colt. He snapped on the lead and walked the colt in circles. Joel gave a little flip of the lead and the colt trotted. Soon the command was made for the colt to slow then stop.

Lolita saw Joel slip something to her colt's mouth, and then a blanket was flipped on the colt's back, and up went Joel, sitting on Chyboon without saddle. She gasped, holding the muck fork midair.

The colt snorted and hoofed the ground then reared. Joel's big frame moved forward and he whispered in the colt's ear. The colt stilled and his ears turned in to the voice. Lolita had never seen anything like it. She thought, *Joel is a natural with horses. Even they surrender to his ways.* She hadn't realized she was daydreaming and dropped the muck until Joel now stood beside her and said, "I'll call A & G's and arrange for a meeting. I'd like you to make the trip with me."

She only nodded and hurled the fork harder than necessary.

Joel went about feeding and watering the remainder of the horses. He stopped at the fence to view the old mare in the pasture, and chuckled. Her filly was closely behind and kicked and hopped and took off running and dashing across the fenced area. As Joel turned, he waved good-bye to George, then pulled his shirt over his head and went toward the plantation house. Time: 7:10 a.m.

In the hospital's parking lot, still in his truck, Joel placed the call to the bull owner.

He was sure that the man over the phone would not know he wasn't Felicite. With the call finished, Joel walked with more assurance, making his doctor rounds with his white coat flapping. He was smiling; one, because arrangements were made for a meeting about the bull, and two, he was in his natural element, the hospital. Joel's day was routine. He signed out two patients, wrote x-ray orders for a few, and barked new medicines for a woman having trouble with pain management. As he glided down the corridor, he stopped in and visited with Bob Chambers, who was now sitting at his desk.

"I'm not working, just getting the feel," Bob rushed and said.

Both men had become fast friends. Bob was more like a visional father image to Joel. He had an easy manner and yet he was subtle, while Bob had a slow, firm approach to all business matters.

Joel chuckled and said, "I better not catch you working. You need to be at home resting. What brings you in here anyway?" He sobered. "You having pain?"

"No, Joel. I thought about what you said about adding doctors to our staff. I believe you're right, it's time for the personnel increase. Think you can pursue some of your Northern doctors our way?" Bob lifted his bushy eyebrows.

"What fields in staffing?" Joel stood with legs apart and arms crossed.

Bob glanced up. "Neurosurgery, orthopedics, and an understudy doctor in your department?"

Joel readjusted his pose and said, "I'll let you know within the month."

Bob nodded, and Joel warned him not to stay much longer, and then left the office. Joel's shift ended and he headed homeward bound, and for the first time since he was a child it felt right. His throat suddenly went dry and his heart hammered when he realized Lolita came to mind. She was what made the plantation feel like home. He grabbed the steering wheel for dear life; his hands were shaking. Joel lectured himself about them being only friends and that she was the one forbidden fruit to not pluck. He drove the short distance, willing himself not to dwell on her in a womanly ways, but only kept repeating, "Friend Zone." He was better off keeping his feelings for Lolita under wraps; after all, who he appeared to reflect in the mirror was not the man beneath the skin. Looks could be so deceiving. Mixed thoughts of genealogy, races, cultures, and years of lies came pouring into his mind. He parked his truck and all but ran to his wing. It was not the time or place to rationalize himself as a ten-nation man again. In his suite, he said, "I'm Joel, doctor, and half owner of this wonderful plantation. And maybe never would be the best time to reflect on my past." He stripped off his clothes and turned on the shower full blast, colder and colder, until he was numb. Joel dressed precisely and controlled each step into the dining hall, willed his mind to shut off, pushing his life of disbelief to a hidden part in his brain and in his heart.

George and the helpers were sitting and talking as the food was being passed to their end. Lolita fluffed her dress skirt and motioned him to sit beside her. He steeled his expression and lowered himself to the seat. He smiled and was cool with conversation and listening to the men talk about the fields of cotton and sugarcane and what they needed to do the next day. George instructed his men to check the fences on the south side and on the north side of the plantation. Since the rains had decreased, the cattle would smell water and want to go to the pond area. And that was not allowed. It had too many marsh areas.

George said, "Joel, make any headway with the bull owner?"

"I did. Lolita and I are leaving in the morning right after breakfast, and the deal should be completely wrapped up and us back on the plantation day after tomorrow." Joel glanced over Lolita's way.

Her brown eyes were shooting darts back at him, but she said too sweetly, "What time did you say we leave in the morning? I want to be ready." She stood.

Joel's smile remained, and he stood and held her chair. He reached for her elbow and urged her to walk with him into the drawing room. He turned to George and said, "I'll call you with the success of purchase and I'll swing out to the barn in the morning to get detailed directions. Good night." Joel continued his easy walk with Lolita.

The servant poured Joel his after-dinner drink and asked Lolita what she would like to have served. She bit her lip then calmly answered, "I'll have a vanilla tea, and thank you." She removed Joel's hand from her arm and she felt the hotness disappear. She swung around and locked eyes with his ocean blues and said, "George will think we're an item, not just friends, and the fact that I agreed to go on this trip is so I can be an advocate between you and the A & G owner. You sure know how to shade the truth when you speak." She reached for the teacup and lightly tipped it to her mouth.

Joel snorted then downed his yellowish liquid. He walked to where Lolita stood and said, in a hushed, stern voice, "We're in the twenty-first century, Lolita, get real!"

Lolita sipped and said, "But we're in the South, Mr. Northerner."

He turned on his heel and walked assertively from the room. In the new remodeled kitchen quarters, Joel asked Elsa, the head housekeeper, chief, and cook, "Which young adult servant girl is available for travel in the morning after breakfast as Ms. Lolita Aime's attendant? We'll be gone for two days. Ms. Aime is accompanying me on a business deal for the plantation." Joel leaned in. "I wouldn't want to do any harm to her spotless reputation."

Elsa fluffed her apron and turned sideways and clapped her hands. A midtwenty-something servant girl entered the room. "Jose, this is Dr. Joel Taylor Wright, and son of the late Mrs. Taylor. You, girl, pack an overnight bag and tomorrow after breakfast, yous leave with the master and accompany Ms. Aime. Yous hear?"

She nodded and braved a brown hand forward. "Pleased to meet ya, sir." Jose smiled and her teeth glistened, whiteness.

Joel lightly squeezed her hand and said, "Thank you for keeping Ms. Aime company on our business trip." He dropped his hand and watched as the young adult scurried from the room. He caught Elsa's brown eyes and said, "Thank you for your help." Joel bowed then straightened and left the kitchen. In his room, he muttered, "Southern ways, reputation, added responsibility. Why couldn't Felicite be here, and why hadn't he answered his cell phone?" He placed another call, voice mail.

The next morning, Joel revved his engine and helped Jose into the backseat, placing her tote bag in the back. Lolita's eyes widened as he introduced them, stating, "Jose is your attendant."

She felt the chill run clear up her spine from his clipped words. That Mr. Northerner, but then Lolita realized he saved her reputation.

Joel placed a classical CD in the slot and said, "Buckle up, ladies."

Several hours later, Lolita stretched out the road map and began with index finger tracing their journey and said, "Joel, watch for the fork in the road and a sign reading Next State." She peeked his way and continued, "And no, it doesn't say what state. One just knows."

He chuckled and adjusted his Stetson, shielding his eyes. He asked Jose what music she liked and all she did was giggle. Lolita said, "Spirituals, that's what Jose's folks sing."

"Great." Joel turned the CD off and said, "Jose, I'm listening," and smiled, showing his dimple.

To Lolita's surprise, Jose began singing and Joel joined in and punched Lolita's arm. "You too, sing."

Joel saw a sign-posted road rest. Several hours had passed and he needed to stretch. He helped both ladies down and went in a different direction. When he returned, Lolita had a picnic table spread with food and drink, and stood swaying in a swooshing dress with that wonderful smile. His body automatically responded to her. He steeled his steps and mentally and consciously warned himself off from these feelings, and forced a smile and a wave.

Joel sat on the same side as Jose and listened as the ladies spoke. He gave a nod or two and enjoyed the plantation cook's prepared meal. He smacked his lips more that once and the iced tea quenched his thirst. After eating, Lolita and Jose quickly cleared the table and stood by Joel's truck. He offered his hand in aiding the ladies in the truck and was glad for the air-conditioning. The afternoon promised to be a hot one. Joel looks at the map and saw the fork was not too far away. Only his finger had touched hers and his lingered.

Jose drew Lolita into a conversation, and Joel gripped the wheel and moved on down the road. It was almost dinner time, 6:00 p.m. Lolita said, "Dr. Wright, we'll be at the cattle farm within the hour, so we might want to find our motel for the night so that would be settled."

Jose scooted forward on the seat and said, "Dr. Wright, some places here still don't hold forth to a darkie staying." She settled back in her seat.

Joel glanced over and caught Lolita nodding her head. "What the..."

Lolita said, "Not everyone in the South agrees that the slaves should have been freed, and then again you have the people prejudiced about skin color and that has nothing to do with slavery, just the color of the person's skin. Aren't people like that up North?"

Joel quickly thought of how his whole life's background had been protected. He could only bob his head.

Lolita said, "I myself, mostly, am not judgmental of what or who a person is. It's his or her actions that tell the story. However, I enjoy the deep Southern ways of the plantation." She pointed. "There a motel."

Joel swaggered into the office, much more confident than he was. He touched the bell on the desk and waited for a person of interest to show. A tall, rounded man came to the counter. Joel hoped there'd be no trouble, and asked, "You have any rooms for the night?"

The man said, "Who you have with you?"

Joel spread his legs and crossed his arms. "Does it matter?" He waited, not blinking.

"How many rooms, lad?"

"Sir, any suites?"

The tall man tilted his head and laughed. Then straightened. "We're at the edge of nowhere. Rooms it is."

Joel lifted his charge card and said, "I'll take three on the same floor."

The man said, "Joel Wright," and narrowed his green eyes. "Are you that newfangled doctor hired in Mississippi's that inherited the plantation?"

"I am…"

"Your mother once stayed here when passing through. A wonderful, caring woman." The man handed over three keys and said, "Drive to the back. Your rooms are near the end. Have a nice stay." He ran the credit card through a machine and handed it back to Joel. "If you want food, there's a bar down the way"— pointing—"but not a place for a woman. The food is plenty and tasty. My uncle owns the bar and works there. Here's a menu."

Joel reached out his hand and said, "Thank you for your hospitality," and tipped his hat.

Joel settled the women and carried in their tote bags. He had them bolt the door, and from the truck he placed a call to the bar and ordered carry-out. He went inside the bar; it was dark and more than rustic. A man much like the hotel owner motioned him to the counter and set the boxes of food up. Joel handed over the credit card and then signed at the appointed place. Several saloon women slithered up to him and in another given time may have tempted him, but he was on a mission and had women to feed, and one was Lolita. He again tipped his hat, gathered his things, and hightailed it out of there. He didn't stop until he pounded on Lolita's door. "Open up, it's Joel."

Lolita slid the door open a crack and said, "Jose is in her room."

He shoved the food into her hands and stomped to the other door and pounded. "It's Dr. Wright, Jose, time to eat." He waited for the door to open and walked beside her to Lolita's room and knocked again.

Lolita had made the food attractive in the arrangement. She found glasses and had water in each. She said, "Let's pray," and held out her hand.

Joel was tired and hungry and felt grumpy, but he still had to see the bull owner. After they ate, Joel wanted a hot shower, but knew the drive for the meeting was at least another forty-five to sixty minutes. He didn't know how Lolita always appeared fresh looking. The three, he and the ladies, arrived at the cattle farm. Joel swung down from the truck and before he ambled to Lolita's side he was met by a short, beefy man. "You're not Felicite!"

"Correct. We're cousins."

Lolita and her new sidekick came tearing to Joel's side. "Well, hello, Mr. Lenard. How are you? Felicite had an emergency and his doctor cousin was available and agreed to come. We both are familiar with your stock. Remember when I came with Felicite and he made a deal with you and you both shook hands...? He informed Dr. Joel Wright of this deal and we're here to seal the transaction. Let's take a look..." She moved forward with Jose, looping arms with the cattle owner and smiling.

Joel fell behind the odd trio and answered only when spoken to. At the barn, Joel saw the massive, long-white-faced steer and gave a sigh. He would agree this bull would be the moving forward of the cattle in breeding.

The owner said, "My price changed...It's eighteen thousand dollars." He stood with a foot on the fence rail.

Joel walked over to the holding pen and studied the bull. Then slowly turned and said, "Ms. Aime, we made a mistake in coming."

He shuffled his Stetson and said, "Felicite assured me you were a man of your word. No sale." He reached for a gaping-mouthed Lolita and began walking toward the truck. Jose skipped along. Lolita opened her mouth to speak but then closed her lips into a tight, flat line.

14

"Say, Doctor Wright, is it? Let's not be hasty. What's your deal?" shouted the bull owner.

Joel continued and lifted the ladies up into the truck and dared either one to speak. Joel righted his steps and opened his truck door. He patted his Cranbury shirt pocket and said, "We—that is, Felicite and myself—expect delivery of the bull to the plantation all in for fifteen thousand dollars, not a penny more." He paused on the step-up and under his breath counted to ten.

The owner yelled, "That's robbery to include the delivery."

Joel swung behind the wheel and started his truck engine.

The man threw his hat on the ground. "All right, agreed. Fifteen thousand, including delivery of the bull. You're worse than Felicite."

Joel opened the door of the truck and jumped down. "I'll take the bull's registration papers with me. Here's half of the money, seven thousand five hundred, the balance upon delivery."

The older man said, "Wait right here." In a few minutes the man was puffing and handed over a large reddish envelope. "Registration papers inside."

Joel wanted to look, but the man appeared to be honorable. He handed Joel a note to sign and had Lolita to witness with her signature. She batted her brown eyes at the man and said, "Nice to see you again."

Joel in the truck tipped his hat and turned his truck around. Lolita said, "Where did you get your bargaining skills? I thought we had lost the bull for sure."

Joel's blue eyes darkened. He said, "I always get what I'm after! Felicite trusted in me and sent me for the bull, and that's what I've done. On the other hand, you, well, were a little soft." He pushed a button on the radio and hummed until they reached the motel. He felt her stare all the way. He walked both ladies to their doors and said, "Bolt your doors." He waited. Jose nodded and went in; he heard the lock click. Joel turned his eyes on Lolita, and she said, "Joel."

He raised a hand and barked, "It's late and we don't want your reputation damaged now, do we. Get behind that door now!"

She swiftly moved inside and he heard the lock click. Joel chuckled and walked to his room. He was hot, smelly, and tired. His shoulders were sore and his head throbbed. He turned on the shower and twisted the knob to hot. He dropped his clothes and stepped under the steamy waters. And then Lolita came to mind. He ached again, but lower. He twisted the shower to cold. After towel drying he pulled on his briefs and lay on the bed. Tomorrow would be a long trip back to the plantation with two females. Joel audibly sighed. "Why didn't I make the trip on my own?" He knew why; Joel had planned on getting to know Ms. Lolita Aime better. "Serves you right, ole boy."

His wake-up call came at 5:00 a.m. He hurried into his clothes, decided against shaving, carried his tote over his back, and knocked on the ladies' doors. 5:22 a.m. "Time for us to hit the trail."

Lolita peeked out the door and said, "Where's the fire?"

Jose had her tote and ambled toward Lolita's door. "I'sa help you, Ms. Lolita. The doctor's ready to leave."

Joel walked to his truck and piled his tote in the bed. Time: 5:45 a.m. The ladies came bustling out. He took their totes from their arms and helped them into the truck, then swung their totes in the truck bed. The motel manager handed Joel three black coffees and said, "Thank you for staying."

Joel glanced over the map and switched on the overhead light. "Ladies, keep your eyes out for a restaurant." He turned the switch off and backed from the motel lot and was on the road. Three hours later, Jose said, "Master, um, Dr. Wright, a sign— Fuel Up and Eat."

"Thanks, Jose." He chuckled. He noticed Lolita was sitting prim and proper with hands folded in her lap. He pulled in at the fill-up and escorted the ladies inside. They placed their orders and, while waiting, he slipped outside and fueled up. Inside, the booth was cramped. His leg touched hers and heat traveled up his body. She distanced herself, but it didn't help.

Lolita said, "Felicite will be impressed with your tactics," and forked her food.

"Sure will, Dr. Wright," Jose said and smiled wide.

Joel forced himself to eat and said, "Thank you, ladies, for your vote of confidence." He stood and slid his hat on and paid the woman at the counter, who was eyeing him like a hungry dog. Lolita placed her hand on his arm and the woman glanced away. Outside, Lolita dropped his arm after he helped her into the truck. Jose waited for his hand and thanked him. Joel climbed into the truck and started the engine.

Lolita, in almost a whisper, said, "You, Mr. Northerner, appear to be quite the eye candy in these here parts," and giggled.

Joel drove for hours. Jose had lowered her body on the backseat and was fast asleep. He leaned over and nudged Lolita. "So why the interest in what other women may or may not think of me?" His smile broadened.

"Well, I certainly don't care one way or the other, Dr. Wright."

He rolled his blue eyes and the smile remained. "We're coming to the fork. Would you like to stop for dinner?"

Her stomach gave off a little growl. "Yes, please and thank you."

He drove in silence pondering over her answer. It nagged him, but why? They made an agreement to be friends…But his whole being wanted more. "Jose, we're here at the diner, wake up."

"Oh, Dr. Wright, yous goes on in without me. I's tired."

"Lolita, is your reputation at risk without Jose?"

"I'm perfectly fine without a chaperone." She jumped down from the truck and her dress whished.

In two strides he was beside her and reached for her hand. He pushed on the truck key, locking the doors and leaving the driver's side window a little low. He kept his hand on her lower back as they entered the diner. They were seated, and he ordered a black coffee before the food would arrive. He asked, "Lolita, how do you like the plantation compared to New Orleans?"

"I enjoy the open space, the stars, the sunrise and sunset, and Felicite is all right. I think your and his new business venture will gain momentum with city folks staying at the resort/retreat. Everyone has been hired and in place. Just waiting on Felicite and you to sign on the dotted line to make the business official. Have you heard from Felicite since he went to New York?"

"No, I haven't. I've left several messages myself." Joel stretched out his long legs. "I hope I don't have to go North looking for him." He locked eyes with Lolita and said, "Felicite said he was to see Jewels in New York, so maybe she's the reason he's out of reach." Joel grinned then chuckled.

Lolita dropped her fork. "Does the hookup bother you?"

"Why should it?"

"Don't you have feeling toward that woman?" Lolita shifted in the booth.

"No. There's someone else that's under my skin." He ran a finger along her neck. "That person is you, if you were wondering."

Her face neck up went red. Unknown to him he meant a whole lot more to her than a possible casual fling. "Joel, I need to get back to New Orleans. I'll leave tomorrow. The website is up and just needs a button pushed and you're all in business. Mom says she doing well, but I don't know with the doctor coming to the B & B almost every day."

Joel straightened and changed his mind's gears. His mouth tightened. "So when will you be back for riding your colt and all, and, Lolita, how much do I owe you for your time and work put in on the resort/retreat project?"

He stepped outside to check on Jose.

She ordered another dessert, chocolate pie. She thought, *There's no need to even give Joel a thought. He's so selfish, that man...*

Joel surveyed Lolita as he came in through the diner door. She was so caught up in thought. Was she missing home? Had she realized their attraction was one of faded lust and not for the long haul?

She glanced at him with that million-dollar smile which lit up her beautiful brown eyes. He went weak in the knees. That woman. He returned the smile. She rose and he ordered a black coffee to go, several sweet rolls, and two iced teas for the ladies, and paid the bill. Back in the truck and out on the road, Jose said, "Um, Dr. Wright, I'm hungry."

Lolita passed the sweet rolls back to Jose and handed her the sweetened iced tea.

Joel remained silent until he saw the road rest sign and said, "Ladies, stretch your legs. I'll meet you back at the truck."

Lolita caught up with him and pulled him inside the building. "Joel." She ran her hand up and down his arm. "To answer your question, I like it at the plantation just fine and could spend my life there, and I'll certainly miss my colt, but it's you I need to distance myself from, because you're like a fine wine that I want but have to limit." On tiptoe, she kissed him lightly and blew on his lips and turned in a different direction.

Joel couldn't move. His whole being wanted that woman. He mumbled, "How am I going to let her leave the plantation and move on without me?" Joel finally walked to the men's area and splashed cold water on his face. Minutes later, he was beside his truck, waiting for the ladies.

It was late when they arrived at the plantation. Joel helped Jose down from the truck and handed her tote and said, "Thank you for attending to Ms. Aime on this trip." He turned and helped Lolita down and whispered, "Thanks for nothing, but being a pain in the…" He left her standing and walked with a purpose to the house. His cell phone was ringing. "Hello, this is Dr. Joel Taylor Wright."

"This is Bob over at the hospital. I need to see you in the morning, say, 5:00 a.m. Sorry I've called so late. You know the walls have ears."

"I understand. I'll be in your office by 5:00 a.m. Good night, sir."

Lolita was standing beside him. "Anything wrong, Joel?" Her voice seemed sincere.

"No. Just necessary business. Thanks for asking." Joel continued up the stairs and went straight to his wing, but not before hearing familiar voices. Joel showered, shaved, and dressed in country casual clothes and combed his hair. "Way too long." Joel descended the stairway two at a time and hurried into the dining hall. "Felicite, when did you get back? I've called and called and now you're here." Joel turned on his heel as he heard a woman's voice. "Jewels?" His eyes bulged and his arches reached his forehead. "Someone pray tell me what's going on at this late hour." Joel placed his hands on his narrow hips.

Felicite stood and crossed over to where Jewels stood. He reached for her left hand and held it up, beaming all over his face. "We're married."

"What?" came Lolita's screeched voice. "I thought you were waiting on me." She took her fisted hand to her heart.

Both Jewels and Joel said, "Felicite?"

Felicite walked over to Lolita picked her up and swung her around and kissed her on the cheek. "Ah, that was before my cousin arrived."

All eyes were on Lolita. She knew he was joking, for they were always just the best of friends, never anything romantic. Lolita said, walking over to Joel and batting her brown eyes, "I'm so busted."

Joel looked at Lolita and then at Felicite. Jewels grabbed onto Felicite's arm and her green eyes were smoldering. Felicite just patted Jewels's hand and walked from the room with her toward his suite's wing, whispering sweet nothings…

The housekeep fluffed her apron and said, "Set down, Dr. Wright, and eat."

He sat and did eat. Lolita with her long shiny hair sat across from Joel and after a bite, said, "What do you make of that?"

Joel's fork hit the china plate and bounced. His blue eyes were in slits. Joel said, "I thought you and Felicite never had a thing? I even asked him," raking his blond hair.

Lolita remained seated and calm. "Now, Dr. Wright, why should you care if Felicite and I have ever been an item or not?" She stood and her dress swished as she walked toward the hallway.

Joel reached her and pulled Lolita into him, bent, and soundly kissed her. He raised his head and stated, "Well, I do." Not letting her loose, he added, "I'm tired of this back-and-forth badgering with one another. Wait here." He all but ran up the steps to his wing and moments later returned and handed Lolita his diary of disbelief. Joel belted, "Read this, then tell me if you want the whole ball of wax—picket fence, marriage, and kids—with me." He kissed her firmly and left her standing staring after him, holding the aged diary in hand.

The next morning, Joel carried a mug of black coffee to his truck, dressed in his Northerner clothes, and headed to the hospital. Something had told him to pack a suitcase and he had. Bob met with Joel and said, "I need you to fly out today and set up meetings with our prospective Northern doctors, and be sure and fly back with them to Mississippi all ready to sign their contracts."

Joel was glad in the distancing, from the plantation, and Lolita, and even from Felicite with Jewels, for a spell. Business was always good for his mind. The plane landed in Columbus Airport and Joel hailed a cab. At the OSU entrance, he met as planned with the potential doctors. Joel knew each of them from bumping shoulders at the hospital. The three doctors were single and practiced in three different doctorate fields—family doctor, Siles; pulmonologist, Dyer; intern cardiologist, Levin. Joel held the cab door open for his colleagues and then got in. Joel told the driver to take them to the Southern Hotel. The men set back and chatted about the weather and its changes and then shared what nurses were now available on the hot date line. Only Lolita flashed in his mind.

At the restaurant, they ate the menu special, meat loaf, mashed potatoes, and green beans, served with black coffees. Joel listened as the men raved at the meal. Joel could only nod and drink his coffee, trying to force down the food. In such a short time he had become spoiled to the real Southern cooking. Joel said, "Bob, the human resource man in Mississippi's hospital, is a fair man. After you read your proposal, gentlemen"—crossing his leg over his knee—"ask me your questions."

Dyer stated, "You seem so settled and, if I say so, happy. Personally, I wagered a few bills that you'd not stay in Mississippi."

Siles glanced up. "What about those Southern women? Do you have the corner on them?"

"Siles, Siles, Siles. I've been too busy to give much thought to the females."

"Right. We know your work ethic or we would not have agreed to meet with you," said Levin. "But we also know you're not shy when it comes to women. And we've heard them talk also—Dr. Wright's eyes are blue as the sky. He carries himself so assured. And he oozes with money."

"Knock it off, men. I'm a changed man." Joel shook his head and chuckled.

Dyer said, "Are checks paid weekly?"

Joel straightened. "Yes, that was one nice perk. Not as much taxes taken out as monthly."

"How about housing? I see the allowance, but is finding a condo easy?" Levin asked.

Joel spurted his coffee. "You're thinking Northerner. On my plantation I have one- and two-bedroom furnished bungalows you can rent out until your housing is secure." He stood and said, "I need to make a phone call. I'll be right back. Here's the website to scout out the places." Joel went to the men's restroom and in the lounge called Lolita.

Third ring, she answered, "This is Lolita, how may I help you?"

"This is Joel. I have three colleagues who may be inquiring about the bungalows through the website. Can you take care of their requests for housing? And it would be nice to plan a trail night with the open fire and some live entertainment."

"Joel…You mean by 'live entertainment,' dance, and with single gals?"

"Yes," he croaked.

"Oh, they've booked three of the cabins. So you've hooked them to come South. Good job! Any of the doctors wanting to settle down?"

Joel blew out a held breath and said, "You never mind about these doctors that are coming back with me. You and I have to talk." He hung up the cell phone and was fisting and unfisting his hands. He wanted a stiff drink fast.

At the table Joel said, "Great offer on the table. Takers?"

All three doctors said together, "When do we leave?"

Joel glanced down at his cell phone and said, "We can take flight tonight."

Three heads bobbed up. Siles said, "Some of us need to list our condos, give notice at work, and pack."

"If I know you three, that's already a done deal. You don't fool me any—you want to bring on the womenfolk for old time's sake." Joel laughed. "All those, dear Johns, I mean, dear Janes to say farewell to."

Dyer nodded and smiled. "Say, why don't the four of us hook up with our flavor of the night at Roadhouse? They have live dancing and rooms are available to close the deal, if any are to be made." His eyebrows lifted up and down.

Joel really wanted to get a hotel room and sleep alone until time to leave in the morning, but Bob's words still lingered. "Don't let up and stay right with them and bring them home." He said, "What time you want to meet up?"

The men looked at each other, and Levin said, "By the time we get to the Roadhouse, our ladies will probably beat us there and be waiting to party. Since we're ready for the evening, let's roll."

The men stood and slapped Joel on the back. He walked out with them and hailed a cab. Joel looked out the window and thought, *I was one of them once, like a cat on a hot tin roof. It seems like a lifetime ago.* He turned toward the men and said, "Our flight leaves out is at 7:30 in the morning."

The night dragged on and Joel limited himself to Coke only, but the men had no clue. They were too busy honeying the women. Joel danced with one of the barmaids several times to throw the men off, and he never held the lady too close. But he couldn't shake feeling that he was cheating on Lolita. What was that? Time: 2:30 a.m. Joel paid for the women's taxi and smoothed their hurt feelings that the doctors were shipping off for unknown parts of the world. He shook his head as he shoved the doctors into a cab and took them back to the Southern where he had booked a suite. Joel slept on the floor, letting the men take the bed and sofas. The doctors were out before he was through with his shower. Joel found himself praying, "Thank You, Lord, for saving a wretch like me." Lolita's face moved before him. He turned the water to cold and questioned, "What if after reading the diary, she never speaks to me again?" Then he broke into a sweat. But what if she did want the picket fence and he was it?

15

JOEL ORDERED THREE pots of strong black coffee to the suite. He directed each doctor to the shower and advised them to turn the cold water on full blast. After uncounted cups of the hot black liquid in the doctors and several rushed trips to the restroom settling their stomach, Joel handed each one their smart phones and said, "Here's the address. Have your luggage forwarded by flight." Joel sat and ate a breakfast of eggs, potatoes, sausage, and toast. He inwardly chuckled for the men still seemed a little green under the collar, so to speak.

"Joel, how do you burn the candle at both ends? You're at least five years older than us," Siles said.

Joel just shook his head and forked another hefty bite.

The cab was waiting out front the Southern for the four doctors. The aspirin bottle was passed around freely. Joel gazed at the men and inwardly said, *I'm so tired of living in the fast lane.* And thought, *In a weird way, I silently thanked my deceased parents for their surprise of the old diary and the plantation that's given me an option to invest in living my life another way.*

At the airport, Joel was the only one with a suitcase and, for that matter, the only one who had changed clothes. Levin said, "We'll need to clean up and have our clothes cleaned before meeting with…Bob, you say?"

"Your packed luggage was air-freighted after you made the call. It should be at the bungalows when we arrive."

Dyer said, "Man, I don't know how you do it," shaking his head.

Joel said, "Men, you give me too much credit," and chuckled.

Lolita met Joel at the plantation house, and he introduced her to the other doctors.

After they all ate she sweetly said, "Men, if you'll follow me I'll show you to your temporary dwellings. And your luggage has arrived." The men stood and all but fell over themselves following her. Joel stepped forward and flashed her a questioning look, and she smiled. He offered her his arm and audibly sighed when she looped her arm over his.

The doctors straightened and used their business manners. Each one was shown their place of stay. Lolita stepped out from the bungalows and Joel joined her. He said, "Thanks for making their arrangements. Was I that much of a greenhorn?"

She clapped her hands. "Was?"

"Now, Lolita, I've came a long way since I first arrived here at the plantation." His hands on hips.

She grabbed his hand and said, "Tomorrow afternoon I've arranged a trail ride, a cookout, and a hoedown, women and all." She squeezed his hand. "Did you want female company then too?"

Joel straightened. "Did you read the diary I left with you?"

Just then, the three men came outside. Levin said, "What time is our appointment with Bob tomorrow?"

Joel turned and forced a smile. "I'll take you all over in the truck after six o'clock breakfast." He turned to walk toward the plantation house and over his shoulder added, "I wouldn't look at the stars too long, men. We have a big day and evening planned."

"What?" said Dyer.

Joel continued, "We'll talk in the morning." He held out his hand to Lolita and quirked a brow. "Coming?" He stood more assured than his stomach was acting.

As usual, breakfast was delicious. The three doctors raved and were friendly in talk with Felicite. The doctors learned quickly to stand when a woman entered the room and to watch their mouths. Joel properly introduced his cousin and his wife, Jewels, and with arm around Lolita reintroduced her by first and last name. George led in saying, "I got a call. The bull should be here this afternoon. Heck of a deal, Joel. That man is still steaming."

All eyes were upon Joel, including Felicite's. Felicite said, "George, you know we are hard bargainers when we want something. It's in our blood." His brown eyes slid to Jewels and then back to Joel and Lolita.

George stood and, on his way out, flopped his hat on his head and said, "But I think Northerner Joel outdid even you, boss," and chuckled.

Felicite kissed Jewels and whispered, "I'll try and be in early."

Lolita said, "No need to rush, Felicite. Jewels and I have a lot to attend to today."

Felicite stopped in midstep. Joel whirled around from the doctors, placed his hands on his hips, and said, "Men, I'll meet you at my truck." He waited until the men, including George, were out of hearing, then Joel continued, "So what do you ladies have planned?"

Jewel moved by Lolita and tipped her pug nose. "Girl's talk." Jewels glanced at Lolita and they walked toward Lolita's room.

Felicite shrugged his shoulders and hurried his steps to catch up with George, and yelled, "Good luck today, Joel."

Joel fidgeted with his tie and headed to the truck. He grabbed his black Stetson and was glad he wore his cowboy boots. He pressed the unlock button and swung into the truck and started the engine. The doctors climbed in and Siles said, "It's not even daylight and everyone is in a bustle for this being a Southern state."

Joel shifted his look and said, "Men, later this afternoon you're in for a real treat. You'll be meeting up with some local gals." He wiggled his brows.

Dyer nodded, and Levin said, "Well, if they look like the examples we've seen, let's sign on the dotted line and bring on the fun…"

The men said, "Hear, hear," and they laughed.

Joel parked in his assigned spot and joked with the men on the way into Bob's office. Bob held out his hand and gave a hearty shake, and had his assistant to bring in five iced teas. "Close the door and hold all calls until further notice. Doctors, have a seat."

Back at the plantation, Lolita and Jewels got acquainted—really acquainted. Lolita wanted to know the ins and outs of one Dr. Joel Taylor Wright. Jewels mentioned, "He's charming, polite, educated, and quite the dancer," and, raising her green eyes, "And Joel's attentive to the woman he's with, and money is never an issue to him. But love—ah, love—no, that was never offered or in the equation. Joel never cared that much, but boy is he ever protective of you, and the way his blue eyes smolder and watch over you. I think you've snagged him good." Jewels giggled.

Lolita bunched her full lips and said, "I just don't know when to take him serious. I'm not sure if I should stay here and help with the resort/retreat and see if Joel makes himself clear, or just go back to New Orleans. That where I'm from. My mother owns a B & B."

Jewels said, "Let me make a suggestion. Joel seems to be waiting for a clue or sign from you, as in the Monopoly game to pass 'Go.' If that is the case, be completely honest with him in your answers. Do this where the two of you will not be interrupted and give nothing of yourself away. You seem very religious. Tell him of your deep faith and your expectations if he's the one." Jewels touched Lolita's hands. "If Joel isn't the man you want and he's not worth fighting for, then don't stay around. Hightail it back from where you came. Joel is too solid of a man for you to toy with."

Lolita air-kissed Jewels on each cheek and said, "I need to change and make sure the event for this afternoon and evening go off without a hitch."

Jewels's eyes widened. "What's the event?"

I've put together an afternoon and evening of fun at Joel's request, for the doctors to go on a trail ride, a cookout, and a hoedown with local gals as a welcome to the South."

"Lolita, can Felicite and I come? It will be our first party to attend as man and wife. What does a gal wear to these shindigs?" She opened Lolita's door and said, "I have to check my closet and, and tell Felicite."

Lolita started out the door of her room, but sat back down and reached for the aged diary. She carefully reread page after page noting, "So the doctor Joel's background isn't squeaky clean, and there may be a closed trunk or two, three, four, five—well, it doesn't matter about the skeletons in the closet or the junk in the trunk, although the penned words are…wow, leaves a person in disbelief. But the information doesn't change the fact, or make or break the person Joel is today." She placed the diary on the nightstand and had to hurry. She changed into her outdoor clothes, slipped on her red cowgirl boots, and went outside. The time had slipped away. Joel and the men would soon be there. She felt weak. She fingered the silver cross on her neck and sent up a quick prayer. "Guide me."

That night was outstanding. The heat was gentled by a light breeze every so often and the horses were cooperative on the trail, although two of the doctors had never ridden a horse, not even at the children's fair.

Felicite received a call from his wife about the event and was able to join in. At 3:15 p.m., he gave both Levin and Siles a lesson in mounting and holding the reins, and had George bring out old Daisy and another retired mare for the two men. The horses were so used to the trail they practically led themselves.

Time: 4:30 p.m. Joel gathered the men and the local women who came to meet the new Northern doctors, with Lolita, Felicite, and Jewels, including George, the cook, and the few men for trail riding in a circle and said a prayer. "Watch over us as a group and individually, help us to enjoy the fellowship and the heavenly design." He squeezed Lolita's hand.

Felicite helped Jewels up on her horse and said, "Mount up, boys and girls," and chuckled. The trail lasted for several hours out.

Time: 6:45 p.m. All dismounted. The cook had gone on ahead to prepare. When everyone heard the iron triangle ring they made their way to the tent. Laughter was in the air and the three seemed to be enjoying their time with the woman who volunteered to join them. Jewels carried conversation all around, and Felicite openly flirted with his wife. Lolita needed to talk with Joel, but no opportune time arose.

Time: 8:05 p.m. Joel said, "Mount up. Dancing back at the resort/retreat grounds." He rode his horse next to Lolita and said, "Save a dance or two for only me?" and his smile lifted. He adjusted his Stetson and kicked the horse in the sides.

Lolita knew she'd have to wait for conversation. She sided up to one of the local gals and asked, "Having a good time and mouthed what do you think of your doctor?"

The woman giggled and reached over and touched Siles's hand, batted her eyelashes, then took her reins in hand. He glanced Lolita's way and mouthed, "Hot...," and smiled.

Lolita knew that feeling, but besides Joel's handsomeness and being all man, she realized she was more than smitten, she was in love with him...How did that happen and so quickly? What would Mother say...?

"Lolita."

She turned, and Joel said, "You all right? You've fallen behind on the trail."

She knew her face was red from letting her mind be distracted about him. Lolita said, "It's nice that you noticed."

"Oh, I noticed, all right, about everything. Are you interested in Siles?"

She belly laughed and couldn't stop. If he only knew...

At the barn, the horses were handed over to George and the men to groom. Time: 9:10 p.m. The music stirred and the hoedown began. The three doctors were out of their element. Joel remembered the time he had been. He sidled up next to Lolita and said, "Suppose the dance could be switched to line dancing to help the poor Northerners out?"

She nodded and whispered into Felicite's ear. The music changed somewhat and the announcer said, "Line dance."

Lolita motioned the gals to lead upfront and have the men follow their step in the rows behind them. Felicite and Joel helped the men, and soon George and some of the hired hands joined in on the fun. It didn't take the city slickers long to change their style.

Lolita had arranged for the cook to bring his wagon and have open service and drinks until midnight. The dance announcer said, "Last dance for the night, ladies' choice."

The three doctors were out on the floor in no time, and so was Jewels and Felicite.

Joel leaned against the barn post and discreetly watched. The music slowed, and a tap came on his shoulder, "Hey, Northern cowboy, want to dance?"

He'd recognize that voice anywhere. Joel turned, bowed, and offered his arm. Lolita accepted. They went from proper handheld to her having her arms around his neck and his hands at her waist. His head was bent so he could capture her every word. Joel tugged her closer to where their lips were just a breath from touching. He couldn't help but inhale her perfume and its sweetness and her. She pulled at the back of his hair, and Joel remembered he hadn't got it cut and it was curling. He dipped her as the dance ended. "Meet me later in the parlor." He lightly grazed her full lips, then walked over to the wagon and helped the local ladies on. George volunteered to take them to town.

Time: 12:45 a.m. The three doctors were trying to get phone numbers, and George said, time to "giddyup." The horses snorted and their ears turned in, as if waiting for the next command.

Joel stood by the men and said, "Tomorrow is Sunday, church at 10:00 a.m. No work or activities, just the community's fish fry that follows the service. Local gals will be there." Joel smiled.

Levin just groaned, and Siles said, "Come on, Levin, Dyer." And Siles walked with them to his bungalow, bidding them a goodnight.

Joel searched the grounds and Lolita was nowhere in sight. He kicked at the dirt and headed for the plantation house. He went to his wing, showered, shaved, put on his expensive cologne, and dressed in black jeans and a Cranbury shirt. Time now 3:00 a.m., Sunday morning. Joel quietly walked into the drawing room; it was empty. A male servant entered and said, "May I pour you a drink, Dr. Wright?"

Joel nodded, and the drink was poured, the bottle was sat down, and the servant bowed and walked backward, closing the missionary door. Joel sipped the yellow liquid. It burned going down his throat. He paced for a while, then sat in the massive leather chair and crossed his leg over the other knee. He took another sip and closed his eyes thinking of the CD and the words penned in the diary; so much of the past story had proven true about his great-grandfather's life, even down through the ages to his own father. And not leaving out the history of his mother's background. Yet it seemed so unreal, and to be blindsided at his age and left without either parent to question. Now, his life's past was so unbelievable, but seemingly true.

Joel sipped again, then set the glass down and hung his head, folding his hands, twiddling his thumbs. He said, "I'm a good man, I work hard, I'm educated, wealthy, proud. I have made a successful new life for myself in the South, and I'm well respected."

He uncrossed his legs and straightened and found himself praying, "Lord, You created me and wrote on my heart while I was still in my mother's womb. What love…" He sniffled.

After a few minutes, Joel carried on, "Thanks for my parents and their upbringing and, not to say, for the materialistic life and privileges given to me, but what I cling and treasure most is being acquainted with You, God. Your grace and mercy and the giving of Your only begotten Son so that someone like me could be saved. What love…It's hard to comprehend." Joel moved from the chair and on bended knee wept, "So, Jesus, here I am naked spiritually before You, presenting my past, present, and future sins, forgive me…I want to be a child of the king." He rose to one knee and added, "I would like Your help with a certain woman to make my wife. Her name is Ms. Lolita Aime. Let me prove to her my trustworthiness as a man, a provider, and as a leader in spiritual things. Amen."

As Joel began to lift, warm arms went around his waist and the voice was crying. Joel blinked. It was Lolita. "Oh, my dear man, how I love you. I slipped into the room and stopped in my tracks as I heard you fighting through yourself. I would say I'm sorry, but I've been honored to listen in. Yes, I will marry you!"

Both clung to each other and kissed and cried, and hugged and prayed some more, until sunrise had ventured the day and all matters humanly, physically, spiritually had been settled. Lolita dropped her hands and said, "I'll be down shortly to attend church with you. I just need to freshen up."

Joel kissed her soundly and slipped to one knee again.

Unknown to either Joel or Lolita, the housekeeper was wary, for neither person, Joel or Lolita, had come out from the drawing room since they had entered it in the wee hours. So she summoned Felicite. There stood Elsa the housekeeper, the plantation staff, George, and the hired men, the three doctors, Stiles, Levin, and Dyer, along with Felicite and Jewels. Felicite quietly held his hand up, and everyone held their breath and paused in time.

Joel, looking up in her brown eyes, said, "I love you, Lolita, with all my heart and I've fought it since the first day we met here at the plantation. You're everything to me, my air I breathe, my being in life. You've touched my soul in a way no other human has or could." He brought out a blue velvet box and flipped open the lid; a diamond bigger than anything sparkled on its white-gold prongs, solitaire setting. Joel let the tears drop from his face and said, "Marry me, sweetheart, my Lolita, be my wife for the rest of our lives."

Lolita saw the crowd and reached out for Joel's arm and said, "Get up."

"No, Lolita, not until you say yes to marrying me…"

Lolita's face was red and tearstained and yet laughter bubbled out. He stayed kneeled, waiting, not moving or saying a word. Lolita saw Felicite nod, and Jewels holding her hands to her own heart with a teary face, and the crowd started hooting, and someone said, "Come on, give the guy a break!"

Joel's blue eyes were pleading and his face sober and hand with boxed ring reached upward. Lolita touched the ring and yelled, "Yes, Dr. Joel Taylor Wright, I'll marry you."

Joel rose and slipped the ring on her third finger, left hand, swung Lolita around, and at the request of the crowd, cheering and clapping, kissed his fiancée. He said, "When can we marry, Lolita? What?"

The speaker was on. "Hello, Mother, Joel just asked me to marry him and I said yes."

"Are you happy?"

"Mother, I am!"

"Well, I knew it when the Northerner came sniffing around. So, Dr. Joel Taylor Wright, when's the big day?"

Joel chuckled and grabbed the phone. "Mother, that's what I want to know…I'm more than ready."

Everyone laughed, and Lynen said, "You better make it quick, Lolita."

Dr. Levin said, "The bells are ringing at the church."

Felicite held hands with his wife and said, "Doctors, step this way. You can ride to church with us."

Joel kissed Lolita again and said, "Perhaps we can speak with the minister today at the fish fry?"

"Great idea. Maybe his time is available next month. I'd like to be married soon and start a family." Lolita blushed. With held hands she whispered, "We've all had a past, and when our children are born we'll embrace their ten-nation background heritages and just simply love them." She lifted on her toes and kissed his o-shaped lips.

They entered the church arm-in-arm with smiles ever so wide, and promises shooting from both their eyes of enduring love and honesty. Joel said, "I'll love you until death and beyond."

The minister lifted his hands at the front of the church and said, "Will all open the hymnal to page 223, stand, and sing 'What a Friend We Have in Jesus.'"

Joel belted the words in his baritone voice and proudly walked to the front holding Lolita's hand, joining in the pew with Felicite with Jewels. As he sang, Joel observed the three doctors standing beside their newly met local gals, and thought, *Hang on to your hats, men, you're in for a long ride*. He then squeezed Lolita's soft hand and stepped closer to her, and whispered, "You do know I love you with all my heart."